Praise for Hazel Marshall

'Swashbuckling pirates, an unrequited love affair and mystery
magic make this a rollicking read'
Liverpool Echo

'*Troublesome Angels and Flying Machines* is a charming
and highly readable fancy'
TES

'An impressive debut from Hazel Marshall ... this is
old-fashioned fare in the best tradition of adventure stories,
expertly paced and confidently written'
Sunday Herald

'An inventive hoot, fast moving and quite bonkers'
Families SE

'An entertaining and unusual story for younger
readers ... the villains are excellent'
History Teaching Review

'An exciting debut novel ... Intelligently written
and a real page-turner.'
Birmingham Post

Also by Hazel Marshall
Troublesome Angels and Flying Machines

And coming soon ...
Troublesome Angels Race to the Rescue

HAZEL MARSHALL was born in Scotland and has lived there most of her life, with occasional breaks to go travelling. She freelances for BBC Radio and enjoys learning languages and different dance styles.

Troublesome Angels and the Red Island Pirates is Hazel's second novel. Her first was *Troublesome Angels and Flying Machines* and it is where Eva and Blanco's marvellous adventures begin ... and the angels aren't far away either!

Troublesome Angels and the Red Island Pirates

Hazel Marshall

OXFORD
UNIVERSITY PRESS

The author gratefully acknowledges the assistance of the Scottish Arts Council during the writing of this book

OXFORD
UNIVERSITY PRESS

Great Clarendon Street, Oxford OX2 6DP
Oxford University Press is a department of the University of Oxford.
It furthers the University's objective of excellence in research, scholarship,
and education by publishing worldwide in

Oxford New York

Auckland Cape Town Dar es Salaam Hong Kong Karachi
Kuala Lumpur Madrid Melbourne Mexico City Nairobi
New Delhi Shanghai Taipei Toronto

With offices in

Argentina Austria Brazil Chile Czech Republic France Greece
Guatemala Hungary Italy Japan Poland Portugal Singapore
South Korea Switzerland Thailand Turkey Ukraine Vietnam

Oxford is a registered trade mark of Oxford University Press
in the UK and in certain other countries

British Library Cataloguing in Publication Data
Data available

ISBN-13: 978-0-19-272614-8
ISBN-10: 0-19-272614-5

1 3 5 7 9 10 8 6 4 2

Typeset by Palimpsest Book Production Ltd, Polmont, Stirlingshire

Printed in Great Britain by Mackays of Chatham plc, Chatham, Kent

For Cara, Katrine, and Mike—for always being there

The Story So Far . . .

It had been only a few months since Blanco Polo had met Eva di Montini and her angels, Azaz and Micha, but when he thought about it, he felt he had known her for years. And that wasn't always a good feeling.

Blanco had met Eva on board a ship bound for Barcelona. She had been travelling there with her Aunt Hildegard, to be married. Blanco, great-nephew of the legendary Marco Polo, was also on his way to Spain, from Venice. He was off to meet Count Maleficio, a trading partner of his father's, who had promised to help him build a flying machine. Unfortunately, their ship had been overrun by pirates and they had had to jump overboard, then walk the rest of the way to Spain. Unwillingly, Blanco agreed that Eva could accompany him to the Count's castle; and not only Eva, but the two angels who, she insisted, always travelled with her—Azaz and Micha.

Once at the Count's castle Blanco had discovered, to his horror, that the Count wanted to build a flying machine so that he could fill it with firepowder and use it for nefarious purposes. In this, he had been assisted by the Stranger—a man whose name they had never learnt—and a dark angel called Rameel. Blanco had discovered the plan while searching for some letters that his great-uncle claimed the Count had stolen from him the year before. He never did find the letters but he did discover that the Count was using him as part of a larger plan.

Having managed to escape, by leaping from a high tower in the flying machine, Blanco had taken Eva to her fiancé in Barcelona, as he had promised Eva's aunt he would do when they had escaped from the pirate ship. But once there, they realized that Eva's fiancé intended to sell her to the Stranger, who had followed them to Barcelona. Both the Count and the Stranger were still after Blanco and Eva. They had had little choice but to steal away on a ship . . .

Chapter 1

'Can you swim?'

'Well, actually, yes,' said Blanco, trying to look modest and failing. He was quite proud of his ability to swim as he knew that not many people could.

'You see that island there?' The captain of the ship pointed off to the left, where a cliff rose up from the sea.

Blanco nodded.

'Could you swim that far?' the captain asked.

'Of course,' Blanco replied enthusiastically.

'Excellent,' said the captain. He turned to the burly seaman standing behind him. 'Toss him over.'

'What?' spluttered Blanco.

'Toss him over,' repeated the captain, walking away. 'And the girl with him.'

The ship got smaller and smaller until eventually it disappeared altogether.

The water lapping around their feet was warm and a beautiful shade of blue. They were standing on a rocky ledge with only a small climb behind them to take them on to the headland. The sun beat down mercilessly. Eva looked at Blanco but he kept staring out to sea as though willing the ship to return.

'It's gone.'

'I know,' said Blanco, through gritted teeth.

'I'm sorry,' she continued, although, truth be told, she didn't look that sorry.

'Stop saying that!'

'Well, what else can I say?'

'Nothing!' shouted Blanco. 'And if you hadn't said anything in the first place then we wouldn't be here. We'd be halfway home to Venice.'

As hard as she tried to prevent it, Eva couldn't stop a tiny flicker of triumph from curling her lips up. Blanco may have been in a hurry to get to Venice but she certainly wasn't. There was nothing but angry parents waiting for her there. She quickly glanced at him but he had missed her smile, which was probably just as well since he was already in a foul mood. She wrung out her wet dress.

'I didn't mean it,' she said defensively.

'Well, the captain thought you did,' said Blanco, 'and, more to the point, so did his crew.' He glared at her. 'And now we could be anywhere and we're soaking wet.'

'It wasn't completely my fault,' said Eva. 'Azaz told me to say it.'

Micha turned abruptly to the angel sitting beside her.

'Did you make Eva call the captain a squinty-eyed pointy-nose?' she demanded.

'I suggested the squinty-eyed bit,' said Azaz complacently. 'She made up the rest herself. The bit about, if his leadership were as sharp as his nose then he would have a much more successful ship, she definitely made up by herself. I had to get them off the boat somehow. You know that.'

Micha shook her head. 'Oh, Azaz,' she said, 'that could almost count as interference.'

Azaz grinned, unperturbed by what she said, even though the strictest of all angel rules was that they should never interfere in the lives of humans. 'No, no,' he said. 'I didn't make *her* say it. I only suggested it.'

Micha looked at Azaz as he sat on the rocks beside Eva. He was polishing his gold belt as he spoke and his red robes were like a blanket of anemones covering the rock on which he was sitting. He winked at her and patted the rock next to him.

She smiled and sat down.

Blanco continued gazing angrily out to sea, mainly so that he wouldn't have to talk to Eva. They had finally been on their way home to Venice and now they were further away than ever! At least in Barcelona, where they had boarded the ship, there had been other ships or they could have walked home. It might have taken a long time but it could have been done. But to be stuck on an island was something different altogether. What if they never got off?

'Oh, this is hopeless,' said Blanco eventually, turning away from the sea and looking up at the cliff. 'I suppose there's nothing else for it but to try and find someone who can tell us where we are. At least the captain said the island was inhabited.'

Eva bit her lip as Blanco started climbing the cliff and debated with herself whether to tell him the last bit of what the captain had said. Blanco had already been tossed overboard by that point and so hadn't heard him. He had indeed said that this part of the island was inhabited but then he had added, 'By pirates'. She decided not to. Blanco would only blame her. He still had nightmares about the last lot that they had encountered. She started to climb the cliff after him.

'Where are we, Azaz?' she whispered.

'Malta,' he said in his normal voice, knowing that Blanco couldn't hear him.

Eva gave a start and almost stumbled back down.

'What are you doing?' asked Blanco impatiently as he glanced at her. 'Put your feet where mine were. It's not difficult.'

'I just slipped a little,' said Eva in such a subdued tone that Blanco should have known that she wasn't telling the truth. Subdued was not a part of her nature. However, he was too cross to listen to her properly.

'Malta,' she whispered under her breath when Blanco had started scrambling up the cliff again. 'Are you sure?'

'Oh yes,' he said. 'I picked it particularly.'

'I knew it!' said Eva, a little louder. 'I knew you had made me say that to the captain.'

'What?' said Blanco, looking back again.

'I didn't make you,' said Azaz. 'I just pointed it out.'

'Nothing,' said Eva, motioning Blanco upwards. 'I'm just talking to Azaz about something.' She didn't want to tell Blanco where they were. He had mentioned Malta to her before. It was where his great-uncle Marco Polo had visited years ago, after his travels. Marco Polo had travelled further than anyone else ever had in the whole world. Before Blanco had left Venice, Marco had asked him to retrieve some letters that the Count had stolen from him, letters between him and a woman he had met in Malta called Magdalena. Blanco hadn't managed to find them, though. It seemed very strange that it was where they had ended up.

Blanco sighed and continued upwards. He had enough to worry about without wondering what Eva was talking to her angels about. He wanted to go home. He had been away for such a long time. All he wanted now was to get back to Venice and ask his great-uncle for advice. Instead here he was, stuck on a red island.

'And it is red,' he muttered as he finally stumbled over the top of the slope and gazed about him. 'Very red.'

It was also one of the flattest, most barren places he had ever seen. Even whole stretches of the north Spanish countryside through which he had walked had been less barren than this. Everywhere was scrubland and all with a pink tinge, and the sun was *so* hot. Desperately he looked for a tree under which to shelter, but there was nothing bigger than a large bush. He turned round to look down at Eva. She was still muttering furiously under her breath to the angels.

When he had first met Eva, he hadn't believed in them at all and had thought that she was touched by the moon when she said that she had two angels who followed her around. Normally only holy women could talk to angels and no one who had ever met Eva would have thought her a holy woman. But since then he had spoken to Azaz and once he thought he had even seen him.

He reached down and pulled her over the top.

'Isn't it lovely?' she said, with a brilliant smile. 'What a beautiful island! It's a lovely shade of pink.'

'It's red,' said Blanco with a frown, 'and it looks

uninhabited. The captain promised that he wouldn't leave us on a deserted island but I think this one is.'

'Oh, I don't think so,' said Eva. 'I'm sure we'll find someone. Look, there's a church over there.'

'Where?'

'Up on the hill. You can hardly see it. It seems to be made of the same colour as the earth.'

'Well, at least we might get some shade there.'

By the time they reached the church Blanco thought that he might melt with the heat. The only good thing was that it had dried their clothes. Soon they were inside the church and settled into the nearest pew. Blanco was determined that not a drop of sunlight should touch him. Once there he sighed.

'Blanco,' said Eva hesitantly. Was this the time to mention the fact that they were on Malta?

'What?' he snapped.

No, not a good time.

'I think there's someone coming,' she said instead.

Blanco could hear the crunch of stones on the path outside. Whoever it was was slow and heavy footed.

'We'd better hide,' Eva continued, looking round for the best place in which to do so.

'Why would we want to hide? I thought the whole point of us being here was to find someone so that they could tell us where we are and maybe help us.'

'Well, yes,' said Eva, looking nervous. The footsteps were getting nearer. 'But what you didn't hear the captain saying was that this part of the island was mainly inhabited by pirates.'

'What!' cried Blanco, leaping to his feet. 'Why didn't you tell me?'

He grabbed her arm and dragged her behind a pillar.

They were just in time. As the last flutter of Eva's skirt disappeared, the church door screeched open. They could see only an outline in the door as the sun, streaming in behind the person standing there, turned him into a shadow. Slowly he shuffled his way forward, aiming determinedly for the front. His progress was slow and staggered.

'He doesn't look like a pirate,' hissed Eva.

'Sssh! He'll hear you,' said Blanco, as memories of the last set of pirates they had met swept over him. There had been a lot of blood and violence. He really didn't want to meet another one—ever!

The man came level with their pillar and they saw him properly for the first time. He was old and bowed and his hands shook slightly.

'Blanco, he is not a pirate,' hissed Eva, louder than before. The old man gave no appearance of having heard her and continued on his way to the front. 'He's just a harmless old man.'

'You said that about the Stranger,' said Blanco. Eva could only sigh in agreement. The Stranger had seemed such a jolly old man, always smiling and chatting away to her as though her opinion had really mattered. But he had turned out to be evil and so Eva was beginning to doubt her judgement about people. But still . . .

'Blanco, he's leaning on a stick and I don't think he can see very well.'

'Well, let's just find out what he's up to,' said Blanco, who had definitely learnt never to take anyone at face value ever again.

As they watched, the old man shuffled up to a casket which lay across the front of the altar. He bent over it as though in prayer but both Blanco and Eva jumped when he suddenly pushed the lid, which fell to the floor with a thunderous clatter.

'You see,' hissed Blanco. 'He *is* a pirate and that's where he keeps all his treasure.'

Eva rolled her eyes but kept her thoughts to herself.

The old man was now scrabbling about in the contents of the casket. With a small cry of triumph he finally found what he was looking for. With a few more little murmurs of delight he lifted his spoils to his lips and started to gnaw.

'Eurgh!' said Blanco. 'What *is* he doing?'

Silence greeted his question and, with a sinking feeling, Blanco realized that Eva was no longer beside him, which meant she was . . .

'What do you think you are doing?' It was Eva at her most stentorian. The old man jumped and turned to face her, still with his mouth full. Blanco groaned. Now they were in the middle of it. Again.

'Stop laughing, Azaz,' said Micha, trying to stifle a smile of her own.

'I can't,' he said. 'Look at Blanco's face.'

Micha turned to look. Blanco's face was a mix of outrage, frustration, and a little fear. He was popping in and out from behind the pillar as though he couldn't quite decide whether to join Eva or leave her alone.

'This is all your fault,' said Micha. 'I hope you know what you're doing.'

'I always know what I'm doing,' said Azaz, settling himself in a pew and watching Eva. 'I thought you'd know that by now.'

'That is a holy relic,' said Eva, with outrage in every tone. 'Why are you trying to eat it?'

The old man merely stared at her, his jaw still working at the bone of the finger that he was trying to gnaw from the holy relic's hand. He was dirty and unkempt looking. His robes, which looked as though they had once been of the finest materials, were threadbare and tattered and draped loosely on his scrawny body. The eyes, which he had fixed on Eva even as he continued chewing, were red-tinged and staring.

'Stop it!' she cried. When the man ignored her, she moved forward, not particularly keen on the idea of touching either the holy relic or the old man. Just as she was reaching out to grab the bone, her hand was seized from behind.

'What are you doing?' hissed Blanco. 'You can't touch a holy relic.'

'Well, he is,' said Eva, motioning with her free hand at the man, who had turned away from them. The finger was proving obstinate and he was having trouble with it.

'That's got nothing to do with us,' retorted Blanco.

'He's doing it right in front of us. We can't just ignore him.'

'Yes, we can. We have enough problems of our own to deal with.'

Eva ignored him and turned back to the man. 'Stop that!' she said to him. 'Put that down at once!'

Surprised by her peremptory tone the man stopped gnawing for a moment. His teeth remained bared: long, strong, yellow teeth. Then he started chewing again. Eva reached out and grabbed his arm. He ignored her.

'You see,' said Blanco. 'Just leave him be.'

'But . . .'

What Eva was about to say remained unsaid as the church door screeched open once more and a tall woman in a nun's habit came striding up the aisle.

'Put that down at once,' she said in such a strict tone that Blanco dropped his pack and Eva dropped the old man's arm as though it had scalded her. The old man, on the other hand, carried on as before.

A glimmer of a smile crossed the nun's face at the sight of the two stunned faces gazing at her. Then she quickly corrected her expression and frowned. She strode past the motionless pair, hoisted up the casket lid and slid it back on. Just before his fingers were trapped between the lid and the hard sides, the old man let go of the bone he was holding and shuffled back. The nun grabbed hold of his arm and led him past the altar to a door in the back wall. When she had opened it she turned.

'Well,' she said, 'are you coming or aren't you?'

Blanco and Eva followed her through the door and were amazed to find themselves looking down on a small, walled town.

Chapter 2

'Malta!'

The abbess looked surprised at the vehemence of Blanco's response to her reply to his question.

Blanco looked around the room as though searching for a map to prove that she was correct. His gaze finally landed on Eva who was trying her best to look as surprised as he was. It wasn't working. He narrowed his eyes at her but decided he would question her later. He turned back to the abbess who was looking at him with a raised eyebrow.

'Can I ask where you were bound?' she asked.

'Venice,' said Blanco.

'But we're not in a hurry to get there,' said Eva. 'I would quite like to stay for a while, if that would be possible. Only, we don't have any money and . . .'

'That would be perfectly possible,' interrupted the abbess smoothly. 'You are welcome to stay for as long as you like. You will not be surprised to hear that we don't get many visitors here. One thing I don't understand, though, is how you got here.'

'We were thrown off a ship,' said Eva, 'by a very rude man.'

'He wasn't the only one being rude,' said Blanco. 'What *you* said was very rude.'

'What did you say?' asked the abbess, looking

curious. Her face, normally sombre, lit up with curiosity.

'She said—' began Blanco, with a cross look at Eva.

'The point is,' interrupted Eva, 'that we are stuck here until we can find someone who will take us to Venice.'

The abbess had watched their interchange with amusement. They had obviously argued many times before. She told them to wait in the courtyard and said that someone would come to show them where they were to sleep.

'This is nice, isn't it?' said Eva.

There was no reply.

'Blanco?'

'Mmm? What?'

Eva turned and looked at him. They were sitting at the top of the steps leading down into the central part of the convent. Blanco was staring down into the courtyard. Eva followed his gaze. There was a novice, a trainee nun, sitting there. Eva knew she was a novice because her dress was a simple white shift which marked her out from the other nuns who were all much older anyway. Her hair was uncovered and it hung halfway down her back. It was long, shiny, and luxurious and Eva couldn't help contrasting it with the tousled, untidy mop which straggled over her own head and down to her shoulders. She pulled a strand out to look and its mousy blonde colour made her drop it again just as quickly. The novice in the courtyard, who looked about their age, was sitting on a bench, sewing an altar cover, but every so often she would put her face up to the sun and her hair would shimmer down her back like a molten river. Blanco couldn't take his eyes from her. Eva dug him severely in the ribs.

'What?' he demanded crossly, turning to her. 'I don't think I've forgiven you yet for not telling me that we were on Malta.'

Eva opened her mouth to deny this but he interrupted her.

'And don't tell me that you didn't know,' he said. 'You didn't look the slightest bit surprised when the abbess told us.'

'Azaz may have mentioned it,' she murmured, glancing back at the angels, who were standing behind them, 'but I didn't want to worry you until I knew that he was right.'

Blanco still had his eyes firmly fixed on the novice below. 'It's a bit strange,' he said, 'that we should have ended up here.'

'Remind me what happened on Malta,' said Eva. 'I know that your great-uncle stayed here for a while and that he fell in love with a woman and that he asked you to retrieve some letters that she wrote. But how did he meet her? Why are the letters so important?'

'He never told me the full story,' admitted Blanco.

'Do you think he might still be in love with her?' sighed Eva. 'I think he is. Why else would he have saved all her letters.' She was cross that Blanco was still staring into the courtyard. She sighed again, loudly. 'What happened to them? Why didn't he marry her? Do you think she's still here on the island? Maybe we could find her.'

'I don't know. And I'm not sure that we should

go looking for her either. My great-uncle is married to someone else, after all.'

'Oh,' said Eva, disappointed on both counts. She stared again at the novice who was now brushing her hair out with her fingers.

'She's not that pretty,' said Micha in Eva's ear. She and Azaz were now hovering above Eva and Blanco.

Before Eva could respond, the abbess came over to the novice and pointed at them both. Blanco immediately began to smooth down his hair and brush his tunic as surreptitiously as he could. The novice walked over to them.

'My name is Sister Agatha,' she said, smiling only at Blanco. 'The abbess has asked me to show you to the guest chamber.'

'There is one really good thing about being here,' said Eva to Micha as she got up to follow Sister Agatha and Blanco.

'What?'

'At least the Count and the Stranger will never find us. If we didn't know we were coming to Malta then neither will they.'

Micha frowned and looked at Azaz, who shrugged his shoulders.

Luca Ferron was relatively happy. He was back in his luxurious palazzo in Venice, he had virtually all the pieces of the puzzle that had eluded him for so long and all he had to do now was to find the missing section of the legend which would tell him the location of the lapis lazuli heartstone.

Luca Ferron was an alchemist and, like all alchemists,

was trying to find a divine spark to make his experiments work. He believed that the spark he needed was a special lapis lazuli stone called the heartstone. He had first heard the legend decades before when he was travelling as a young man. He had tried to find out more about it but people denied that it even existed and nobody knew where it was to be found. Soon the story faded into the recesses of his mind.

The memory was revived when he met Count Maleficio. They had been drawn together by their shared interest in alchemy and also because they both knew the dark angel Rameel. Rameel was a rebel angel who was interested only in helping humans to create destruction. He could be heard by both Luca Ferron and Count Maleficio, although only Luca could see him.

The Count was also the only other man Luca had ever met who had heard of the lapis lazuli heartstone. He had heard of it years earlier, when he had been living on the island of Malta. There he had fallen in love with a woman who was in love with a man called Marco Polo. The woman and Marco Polo had written love letters to each other which the Count managed to intercept and read as they went back and forth. The Count had discovered that within some of the letters lay a code and within that code lay the legend of the heartstone. Then Marco Polo had disappeared. But the code that the Count had managed to translate from Marco's letters to Magdalena had remained with him for years, shaping his experiments. Being able to fly like a bird and make something that resembled thunder and lightning became his life's work. With these vital elements, he would find the stone.

Twenty years later, while visiting Luca Ferron in Venice,

the Count had come across Marco Polo again. The Count had managed to steal the remaining letters and ever since then, Luca and the Count had been trying to find in them the key to where the heartstone was hidden.

While in Venice Luca had first of all read the part of the code which explained who could free the stone.

To win this stone the Adept must
First of all, fly like a bird,
Speak with the angels
And love like no other . . .

He had stored this in the back of his mind but when he had met Blanco Polo and Eva di Montini at the Count's castle, he had not realized that the Adept was there, right in front of him. It had not been until Eva and Blanco had escaped from the tower that Luca had realized that Eva was the one who fulfilled all the requirements. Thanks to Blanco making her sit in the flying machine she had flown like a bird. She could definitely speak with the angels, better even than he could. And any fool could see that she was in love with Blanco.

But now, with all the letters and with virtually everything decoded, they had lost the girl.

'You have to call me Sister Agatha,' said the novice in a soft breathless voice, 'although I'm not really a nun. My father has only put me in here for safekeeping from the pirates until he can find me a husband. I don't really want to be here.' She had shot Blanco a very flirtatious look as she said this.

'You're in here,' she continued, turning to Eva, her

smile disappearing. She motioned to a room with eight pallets in it. The one at the end had sheets folded neatly on top in a little pile. 'You can make your pallet up while I show Blanco where he is to sleep.'

She turned away and walked off before Eva could say a word. Eva narrowed her eyes as she looked after them. She didn't like that girl. Not one bit. A little spark of jealousy settled in her stomach as she watched them walk away.

That little spark grew bigger in the days that followed. Blanco hardly ever spoke to her. He was always following Sister Agatha around. She was in charge of the herb gardens and so Blanco had offered to help her since they had no money to pay for the guest chamber. That was where Eva found him the following morning when she was sent there by Sister Assumpta.

'Blanco, I have to talk to you,' she said.

He turned round with an annoyed look on his face.

'Can't it wait? Sister Agatha is showing me the properties of the lemon balm plant.'

'It's supposed to help guard against jealousy,' said Sister Agatha, smiling sweetly. She held out a leaf. 'Would you like to try some?'

Eva scowled at her but managed to bite back the rude reply on the end of her tongue.

Blanco looked from her to Sister Agatha.

'We can talk later,' he said to Eva, and turned his back. Sister Agatha gave her a triumphant little smile and then turned her back too.

Eva had gazed furiously at their backs for a moment before stalking off. In addition to being annoyed, the deep dull ache somewhere in her belly region grew stronger as she realized that Blanco liked someone else better than he liked her.

A warm rush from behind her made her stop.

'*What's the matter?*' *asked Micha.*

'That girl,' snapped Eva. 'I hate her.'

Micha looked at her sympathetically for a moment. She knew how Eva felt. She had seen how Blanco looked at Sister Agatha and she knew how much Eva liked Blanco.

'Eva!'

Eva tried to make herself as small as possible. If she could have disappeared into the wall then she would have. But she was soon spotted.

'There you are!' said Sister Assumpta, who was in charge of the kitchens. 'Have you found the sorrel?'

Sister Assumpta had sent her out to find some sorrel for the meat she was cooking but Eva had forgotten to ask for it when she was in the herb garden and didn't want to go back.

'Oh, really!' snapped Sister Assumpta when she saw the empty basket. 'I ask you to do a simple task! I'll do it myself. You go back in and scrub the vegetables.'

Eva was loath to leave the comfort of Micha's wings but Sister Assumpta was staring at her and Micha herself gave her a tiny nudge. She hadn't wanted to go back to Venice but now she was thinking that she would much rather be there than on Malta.

'*What are you up to?*' *asked Azaz, flying down to land beside Micha. She was watching Eva and she had a calculating look on her face.*

'Nothing,' she said innocently.

Azaz tried to look her in the eye but she managed to avoid him by fiddling with her wings.

'I hope you're not going to do anything to that girl,' he said.

Micha lifted her golden head and smiled. 'Me?' she said. 'Of course not.'

Chapter 3

A few days later Eva finally persuaded Blanco out of the convent. They wandered through the streets of Mdina, the town in which the convent was located. It was a small, walled town and it reminded Blanco a little of Venice, although without the canals. But the streets had the same way of twisting away so that it was never clear what lay around the next corner. He supposed it helped in the event of an attack. Those who lived here would know where to go, how to hide, and the best places for ambushes. He frowned. Of course, they would be open to attack from the skies, from the Count's malicious version of the flying machine. He was very glad that it had been destroyed. He smiled to himself. He was enjoying himself in the convent. The Count, the Stranger, and any danger seemed leagues away from such a peaceful place.

Lost in his thoughts he barely noticed that Eva was leading him through the town gates and out into the surrounding countryside.

'Where are we going?' demanded Blanco when he did realize where they were. 'Why do you need to speak to me so urgently? I promised Sister Ag—'

Eva interrupted him before he could say her name.

'It's not a matter of urgency,' she said. 'I just thought we should talk.'

'What about?'

Eva sighed. Sometimes Blanco could be a little bit thoughtless.

'Us,' she said. 'Being on Malta. Magdalena. Getting off this island.'

Blanco nodded slowly. 'I suppose you're right,' he said reluctantly. 'Actually I'm not in such a hurry to go home now.'

'Well, I am,' said Eva.

'Really?' he said in surprise. 'I thought you would do anything not to go back to Venice. I thought that was why you said *that* to the captain.'

'I told you,' said Eva crossly. 'It was Azaz.' She stopped herself from saying anything further about that. Arguing with Blanco was not going to help her case. 'Why do you want to stay?' she asked. She wondered if he would admit to liking Sister Agatha.

Blanco blushed furiously. He couldn't mention Sister Agatha. She was almost a nun, after all. He thought quickly.

'I think we should try and find Magdalena,' he said.

'Oh,' said Eva, taken by surprise. 'Oh, that's a good idea.'

'I thought you wanted to leave,' said Blanco.

'I do,' she said hastily, 'but I think, since we're here, that we owe it to your great-uncle. Since we couldn't find the letters.' And if it meant that it delayed going back to Venice *and* he spent less time with Sister Agatha then even better.

Blanco frowned a little at that. He had only said it to stop Eva asking any more questions. He wasn't sure that he should be digging around in his great-uncle's past. Trying to retrieve stolen letters was one thing but finding Magdalena herself would be an entirely different matter.

'She may be dead,' he said. 'In fact, from the way Gump spoke about her I'm fairly sure she is.'

'It would explain why they didn't get married,' said Eva. 'But I think we should at least ask a few people.'

'I asked Sister Agatha,' said Blanco, 'but . . .'

'You did what?'

'She is from here. I thought she might know someone of that name but she doesn't.'

'Well, it would all have happened before she was born,' said Eva. 'We would be better asking the abbess.' She frowned at Blanco as an unwelcome thought came to her. 'What else did you tell Sister Agatha? Did you tell her about the Count?'

Blanco nodded.

'And the Stranger?'

Blanco nodded again and Eva was struck by a moment of fear. It seemed to come from nowhere, as though just by saying his name she had brought him closer. The stranger had wanted to kill them both. He was still looking for them and for Eva in particular because he had decided that her ability to talk to the angels meant that she had some special power that he needed.

'I wish you hadn't done that,' said Eva slowly. 'It's none of her business.'

'Well, I can't see how it could do any harm,' began Blanco.

They were still walking along and as they crested a small rise Eva suddenly clutched his arm.

'Careful!' she said, pulling him down behind a rock. They were just in time for a moment later a large, swaggering, and very drunk seaman passed right in front of them.

'That was close,' said Blanco.

'Well,' said Eva, nudging him with a sharper elbow than was strictly needed. 'Go on then.'

'What do you mean?' he asked.

'Go and speak to him.'

'What?'

'Go and speak to him. See if he's got a ship and when his ship is due to sail.'

'He's a pirate!'

'You think everyone's a pirate! You're not scared, are you?' teased Eva.

Blanco scowled at her. He wasn't about to get himself run through with a sword just because Eva was taunting him.

'Oh, Blanco,' said Eva, changing her voice from her usual bell-like tones to Sister Agatha's higher whispery ones. 'You're so brave. Talking to a sailor.'

'Oh shut up!' said Blanco giving her a little push.

'Shut up yourself,' she said, pushing back.

Blanco always maintained later that he had been balancing on the wrong leg and that, on a normal day, Eva would never have been able to push him down a slope. But he didn't have time for such thoughts at that moment. All he could think about was how few bushes there were to grab on to as he tumbled head over heels down the scree. He tried not to yell in order not to attract the pirate's attention but couldn't help the odd little whimper escaping from his throat. More to the point, he was catching up with the pirate fast and if he didn't catch hold of a bush soon, was about to overtake him.

Snouty was drunk. So drunk that a few odd grunts, yells, and whimpers from behind him didn't even enter his consciousness. But even he couldn't ignore a tall, slim youth rolling to a stop at his feet.

Neither said anything for a moment. They didn't even look at each other. Snouty wasn't entirely sure that what he was seeing was real. Drinking home-brewed spirits with the local smugglers was a dangerous business and his brain was doubtless addled. Then the youth gave a groan. Even with that proof, Snouty was debating, in a rather slow and deliberate manner, whether he should step over the boy and carry on as though he had never seen him, when he was given an almighty push in the back.

'Don't touch him!' cried a furious voice.

Azaz and Micha were not the only angels on the island. When, along with Eva, they had joined Blanco on his adventures in Spain, they had known that there was a dark angel loitering in the Count's castle. Now Azaz had finally admitted to Micha what she had suspected all along: that Rameel, the dark angel, was on this island and that was why Azaz had persuaded Eva to say what she had to the captain so that they, too, would end up on Malta. He had been looking for Rameel since they had left Barcelona for he knew that he could not be trusted alone for too long without creating havoc.

Azaz and Micha were angels who had fallen through their own choice. Micha had been in love with a human, which was forbidden, but she had chosen to live the length of one human life with him and then become a rebel angel.

Azaz had fallen because he had wanted to teach and was curious about how things worked. But there were other angels who had fallen too, all for their own reasons, and one of them was Rameel. His only reason was destruction. The rebel angels were forbidden to interfere in the plans of humans, yet Rameel ignored this at will and actively encouraged people like the Count in their destructive experiments. So long as Rameel continued interfering, Micha and Azaz would have to spend their time trying to stop him.

'And he's here?' asked Micha.

Azaz nodded. 'I'm almost certain. I haven't seen him yet but I can smell him. I'm sure he's here.'

'I thought as much,' confessed Micha. 'There is a distinct unpleasantness in the air. We should warn Eva. If he's here then so will . . .'

'Let's wait,' said Azaz, 'wait until we're sure.'

Snouty's befuddled brain was still trying to catch up with the fact that there were suddenly two people where there had been none before. One, who had rolled to his feet, was slowly rising; the second, who had pushed him, was still battering his back with blows which, while not exactly painful, were certainly annoying. He reached round and caught hold of his assailant and hauled her round in front of him.

Blanco had been debating whether to make a run for it but when the pirate caught hold of Eva, he had to reconsider. He couldn't leave her there, not when she had come down to save him. Not, he added to himself, that he had needed saving. The pirate was not looking very happy. His little eyes were screwed up tightly with anger.

In truth, Snouty's eyes were like that because the strong sunlight was hurting them. They were throbbing in their sockets as though they had been punched into place that morning.

Eva, meanwhile, was wriggling in his grip until he roared at her to be still. Even then she glowered at him and wondered whether kicking him would be a good idea.

'What are you doing?' growled the pirate.

'We were . . . em . . . just passing,' said Blanco. 'I tripped and fell and landed in front of you and I think my friend here thought you were going to attack me and came down to help.' Blanco spoke in his most cultured tones, thinking to impress the pirate with his breeding and possibly intimidate him into letting them go.

It didn't seem to be working. A wide grin spread across the pirate's face showing hideous blackened teeth—at least in the parts where there were teeth. Most of his mouth was a cavernous, gaping hole.

'Well, ain't you the nicely spoken one,' he said. 'Do you speak like that too?' He gave Eva a rough shake as he spoke.

'Get your hands off me, you big fool!' said Eva. He was gripping her rather tightly and she saw no reason for it.

'Lovely,' he said. 'The captain will be pleased with me for bringing you two back. You'll be worth a nice ransom.'

'What do you mean, ransom?' asked Blanco suspiciously, although he had a good enough idea.

'Why, I'll take you back to the ship and then we'll

send a ransom demand off to your parents and they'll pay us a nice whack to let you go.'

'Ah!' said Blanco, looking smug. 'You'll be disappointed then. We don't live here. Nobody will pay any ransom for us.'

The pirate looked disappointed for the merest moment and then his face brightened again.

'Well,' he said, 'we'll just have to make use of you in some other way. Scrubbing the decks or something.'

Realizing that perhaps this pirate wasn't quite as scary as some of the others he'd met, Blanco began to argue with him. He could see that there was no use in trying to fight him for he was at least twice his size and even if Eva were to help him the pirate could easily hold them both off. He did wonder why Eva wasn't saying anything—it wasn't like her to stay silent so long. But she was just standing there glaring.

'Come on then,' said the pirate, stopping the argument effectively by holding both of Eva's hands with one of his and trying to grab at Blanco with the other.

'No,' said Blanco, jumping out of the way.

The pirate grinned at him nastily and twisted Eva's arm so that she screamed out. 'I'll hurt her more if you don't come along quietly,' he said and Blanco could see that he meant it.

He grabbed hold of Blanco easily and twisted his arm behind his back so that he couldn't fight or struggle any more.

'Now, let's go,' said the pirate. 'My head's aching and I can't wait to get out of this sun.'

'Thanks for all your help,' muttered Blanco to Eva. 'If you'd struggled a bit we might have been able to fight him.'

Eva smiled beatifically at him and then winked. Blanco glared at her. This wasn't a game! A moment later she stumbled.

'I'm so sorry,' she said sweetly to the pirate. 'It's because you're holding both my hands. If you only held one I could walk much more easily.'

Had Snouty not drunk so much the night before he might have been suspicious of the sweetness of her tone. But his head was thudding worse than the sound of a thousand hammers on metal and his tongue felt as though it was at least three times its normal size and swelling in his mouth by the moment. He also wanted to get to the ship as soon as he possibly could, partly so that he could lie down out of the sun and partly so that the captain could congratulate him on the booty that he had brought back. He frowned a little as he thought about the captain's woman. He wasn't sure that she would entirely approve of human booty but, he reasoned, he could always send them away again if she didn't. Meanwhile, the girl was being quiet and seemed resigned to her fate. It couldn't do any harm to let go of one of her hands.

As soon as Eva's hand was free she dug about in her pocket until she found what she was looking for. It was small and round and fitted perfectly into her palm. She closed her fingers round it as she edged it out.

Snouty thought he was being blinded. He had never felt such intense pain in all his life. With a roar he brought up both his hands to protect his eyes.

Eva, having caused the pain, was completely prepared and grabbed Blanco and dragged him off.

'What the—' he started, as they stumbled away, running as fast as they could back up the hill down which he had tumbled not so long ago.

'Shut up,' gasped Eva. 'Keep running.'

She was scared to look over her shoulder in case the pirate was running after them, although she knew it was unlikely. For one thing, she had virtually blinded him and for another, he was far too heavy to run uphill quickly. Still, it wasn't until they reached the top that she looked back, to find that he was stumbling off in the opposite direction.

'What in the name of all the saints did you do?' gasped Blanco from where he lay, flat on his back, breathing heavily.

'I used this,' explained Eva, handing over something small, hard, and round and closing his fingers round it. 'Watch how you open your fingers. Don't open them straight into the sun.'

Blanco slowly unpeeled his fingers and what he saw there made him howl with laughter. It was such an innocent little thing to have caused such pain. It was a little piece of polished metal. A mirror. Eva had shone it into the sun and then reflected it into the pirate's eyes, almost blinding him in the process.

'What are you doing with a mirror?' he asked. 'I never knew you were so vain!'

Eva snatched it back. How dare he call her vain? If either of them was vain, it was definitely Blanco. 'If that's all the thanks I get for saving you,' she began.

'Saving me?' interrupted Blanco. 'If you hadn't pushed me down in the first place . . .'

'I didn't push you—although I'm beginning to wish I had!'

They argued as they walked.

★　★　★

Snouty, thinking about it later, decided that it had all just been a horrible hallucination brought on by the home-brewed spirits. He swore never to touch the stuff again—after just one to recover from the shock.

Chapter 4

The argument was still going on. Suddenly Eva found that she was being blamed for everything, all the way back to the initial incident with the pirates when they had first left Venice.

'You're just trouble, Eva,' said Blanco. 'There's something about you that attracts it. I know it's not always your fault but . . .'

Normally Eva would have argued back but today she felt tired of all the arguing and just wanted Blanco to be nice to her. She felt totally alone. Blanco was looking forward to going home to Venice because Marco Polo, his beloved Gump, was there. Even here, he was enjoying himself with that annoying Sister Agatha. But what did she have? She wanted Blanco to like her more than anything but more often than not he just treated her like something that he had been lumbered with.

Lost in her melancholy and, it had to be admitted, self-pitying thoughts, it took her a while to realize that Blanco had disappeared.

'Blanco!'

She looked around. Where could he possibly be? In the distance she could see the church they'd found on their first day in Malta but everywhere else, empty landscape mocked her. Like so much of the island, the area in which they were walking was barren and sandy. There were no trees, no hills, nowhere to hide. There were only a few straggly bushes.

'Blanco!' she called, quite desperate this time. Was she going to have to return to the convent alone and come back with a search party? Had that pirate doubled back and snatched him?

No. She shook her head as though to clear it of that thought. He couldn't have done it without her knowing and, anyway, Blanco would have put up a bit of a struggle and she would have heard him. He had simply disappeared into thin air. One moment he had been talking and the next he had gone. The more she thought about it, the more sure she was that that was how it had happened. She had been walking ahead, only half listening, immersed in her own thoughts, so it had taken a few moments for the silence to sink in but, yes, he had just suddenly stopped talking. Another thought came to her.

'Azaz? Micha?'

'Snnrgh!'

A faint cry came from behind her.

'Blanco?' she called.

'Snnrgh . . . under . . . Grssh . . . here!' The last word was quite emphatic and Eva realized that it was coming from beneath the bush close to her left foot. She walked over and then nearly fell, as her right foot disappeared from under her.

'Ow!' came Blanco's voice, much louder now and not sounding happy. 'What are you doing up there? You just made lots of dirt fall in my eye.'

'Sorry!' called Eva, as she hauled herself back from the edge of the pit into which she had nearly fallen. She thrust her face down the hole.

'Are you all right?' she called.

'I'm fine. It's amazing. I've never seen anything like it before. There are tunnels here. Come down.'

'Erm,' said Eva, 'I don't think I will, if it's all the same to you.'

'Come on,' he said. 'I want to go exploring.'

'Well, it makes sense that I stay here and make sure you know the right spot to come back out,' said Eva in what she thought was a sensible voice.

'I've got string,' said Blanco. 'We can tie it to one of the bushes here and then follow it back.'

'No, really, you go. I'd only slow you down.'

There was a pause.

'You're not scared, are you?'

Eva *was* scared. Terrified, in fact. She had been scared of dark, enclosed spaces for as long as she could remember.

'Of course not,' she called down. 'I'll just be a moment.'

'What are you doing?' asked Azaz, appearing just as Eva was about to disappear under the ground.

'Blanco fell down here,' said Eva, with relief at seeing them. 'I was going down to join him. He wants to explore. But perhaps one of you could go instead of me?' She looked up at Azaz, who was always first to try anything new, who always knew what to do, and was never scared of anything.

'I can't go down there,' he said without a moment's hesitation.

'You're not scared, are you?' asked Eva, more out of curiosity than anything. She had never known Azaz to be scared of anything.

'Not scared exactly,' he said. 'It's just . . . that . . .' He hesitated, not quite sure how to say it.

'We can't go underground,' said Micha, finally helping him out. 'We're not allowed.'

'Oh,' said Eva. 'I see.' Although she didn't. But it seemed that it was going to be her who went.

She sat back on her heels and pondered the small opening that she was expected to climb into. If only Blanco hadn't asked if she was scared. Eva never could resist a challenge. Taking a deep breath, she placed her feet in the hole and began to feel her way down.

Just before she disappeared completely she looked at the angels who were watching her with worried eyes.

'This isn't the way to hell, is it?'

That made Azaz laugh. 'No,' he said. 'I can promise you that hell is not down there.'

'And we'll be here when you get back out,' said Micha.

Only slightly comforted, Eva was soon far underground. She was terrified that she might find herself facing the devil or one of his demons, although a tiny part of her couldn't believe that she would. After all, everyone knew that the gates to hell didn't lie beneath some barren little island in the middle of the Mediterranean Sea. And Azaz had promised her. Thankfully, the tunnel broadened out quite amazingly. They passed through a series of chambers each larger than the last, each with its own dark little alcoves and further tunnels that Eva just knew she didn't want to explore any further. She thought that they were heading in the direction of the church.

'Ow,' said Eva as she bumped her head on Blanco's back.

'Sorry,' he said. 'I keep forgetting that I have to warn you when I'm going to stop.'

'What is it? Why have you stopped?'

'The string's run out.'

'Well, let's go back then,' she said, trying to keep the relief from her voice. She wasn't sure how she had managed to stay down for so long without screaming. She would probably have permanent marks on the palms of her hands from where she had been digging her fingernails into them and her ribs hurt from the deep gulping breaths she was taking. She could also feel an unpleasant fluttering in her chest and was convinced that the walls were closing in on them.

'Just a little bit more,' pleaded Blanco. 'I'm sure I can hear something.'

If anything was guaranteed to make Eva want to turn back it was the thought that there might be something lurking in these underground chambers.

'I'd rather go back,' she said, glad that the darkness hid her trembling, but praying that Blanco would catch just a little hint of the fear in her voice and turn back for her sake.

'I won't be a moment,' said Blanco and she felt rather than saw him move forward.

'Don't leave me here!' The shout came out much louder than she intended and it echoed round the chamber.

'Well, come with me then,' said Blanco impatiently. 'I'll just put the string down here and we'll only walk in a straight line. I promise that we won't go far.'

Eva didn't believe him. She hadn't heard him this excited about anything since the early days of the flying machine. But she had no choice. Going into danger with Blanco was infinitely preferable to being left on her own.

She followed him closely, slipping her hand into his.

He resisted for a moment and then he tightened his grip and pulled her along behind him. Not far in front of them there was a strange glimmering light, flickering like a candle. Blanco couldn't believe that there could be light this far underground.

Though he would never have admitted it to Eva, he was a little bit scared himself and was strangely comforted by holding her hand. They crept forward slowly and Blanco, as the one in the lead, was the first to look round the corner into what was indeed candle-light.

But it was not one flickering candle that he saw: it was a multitude, and caught in their eerie light was an exact replica of the Count's laboratory as they had last seen it in the castle all those months ago, except this time there were no flying machines. Eva peered over his shoulder and they gaped open-mouthed, wondering if the Count himself might appear. Eva glanced behind her, worried that he might even at the moment be sneaking up on them.

'Blanco,' said Eva hesitantly. 'Does this . . . is this . . . ?' She faltered, not really wanting to continue.

'It must belong to the Count,' said Blanco. 'It must. It looks just the same as his room in the castle.'

'But why would he be here?'

Eva kept glancing over her shoulder, convinced that Count Maleficio was going to appear at any moment. She couldn't believe that he was here, on the same island as them.

'I don't know,' said Blanco slowly. He was worried about the Count, of course. After all, he had tried to kill both him and Eva. But, just looking at all the experiments laid out before him filled him with excitement as well. 'But there is a way to find out.'

Blanco took a step forward and Eva grabbed at him, but just missed. He looked around the chamber with awe.

There were candles flickering in all the little alcoves, held in place by something. Blanco drew back quickly with distaste as soon as he realized that the candles were stuck into the eye sockets of human skulls.

In the light that they threw out he could see all manner of strange instruments. Blanco recognized some of them but others were unusual and he couldn't work out what they were for. The chamber was crowded, although tidy. Bottles, jars, sacks, and barrels of multicoloured sands, stones, and liquids. There was a fire burning fiercely in the corner and another one burning in a furnace. Blanco saw that there was a third burning with a lilac flame. Looking around, and convincing himself that there really was no one there, Blanco went over to look more closely at one of the machines. It was covered in engravings and as he studied it, he took a sharp, indrawn breath. He was pretty sure it was alchemy. On top of all his other sins, the Count was an alchemist. Blanco frowned. He couldn't see any metal for turning into gold. Just what exactly was the Count trying to do?

Eva had followed Blanco into the chamber. She didn't feel very happy about it but she had decided that she would rather be in the chamber with him if the Count appeared than stuck in a dark tunnel. She looked at one of the parchments that were lying open on the table. She wasn't a particularly good reader— her father had thought that education was a waste of time for girls—but Blanco had been teaching her over the past few months.

'Love Potions,' she read aloud. She carried on reading to herself.

For the sick at heart
To cure the sick at heart, first take five leaves from a flowering mountain daisy; add to this some fur from a small, wild deer and the fluff from a rabbit's tail. Place in a tisane of boiled water with the following herbs—feverfew, tansy, spikenard, and monk's bane. Once this is made, add the final ingredient: three tears from a disappointed lover. This potion can be kept for up to thirty years.

For the love rival
Take three dandelions and grind them to a paste. Add a marigold, a primrose, and the whisker of a sandy coloured tom-cat. Stir well together and leave overnight. If added to anything liquid, the taste is almost undetectable. For a week the drinker will be constantly running to the water closet to expel bad humours, thus leaving the field clear for pursuing the loved one.

To make someone fall in love with you
Grind a small ruby with five petals from a rose of the deepest, darkest red. To this add five red berries from the holly tree. Mix with the juice of red grapes and leave to soak for two weeks. When it is ready, add the final ingredient, which is a quantity of your own blood taken from the fourth finger of the left hand. Mix well. This mixture will take effect within moments of drinking.

The last one was heavily marked and Eva could see that many of the ingredients were lying on the table.

'Blanco,' she called. 'Look at this.'

But Blanco was too engrossed in his own parchments. He had found the Count's notebooks.

> To burn with a blue flame, add indigo. To burn with a purple flame, add cinnabar. For yellow ...

Blanco looked further down the page and frowned. It looked as though the Count was experimenting with firepowder again.

> To increase the flash add an extra handful of solvestone. This will create a marvellous combustion and cause even the most brave to cower in fear, for they will know not what dreadful event has overcome them.
>
> In order to achieve the best result in the case of the miniatures, the preferred mix is six helpings of sulphur to one and a half of charcoal plus one of the solve-stone. The best solve-stone is that found in the blue barrel which was sent from Sicily.
>
> I have started to increase the size thereby also increasing the result. To do this I have ...

Blanco turned the page.

Eva had moved along the table and was inspecting a little bowl of white crystals, each about the length of her fingernail.

'Blanco,' she said, picking one up. 'What do you think these are?' As she held it up, it crumbled in her hands. Blanco hadn't looked up anyway. He was staring transfixed at the page in front of him. Eva came to read over his shoulder.

> If I ever see Blanco Polo again, I will kill him.

Azaz and Micha were lazing by the entrance to the hole into which Eva had disappeared when Azaz reached out a hand and grabbed at something. Rameel was suddenly in front of them.

'Could you let go of my wing?' he asked Azaz. 'I've just cleaned it.'

He certainly looked better than the last time that they had seen him at the Count's castle. Then he had looked sallow and ill and as though he hadn't seen sunlight for an age—which he hadn't, for he had been trapped in a pit for centuries. Now he looked much healthier and his long dark hair was shining with health rather than grease. His wings were well groomed and silky to the touch.

Azaz got to his feet and let go of Rameel's wing in the process.

'I knew you were here,' he said resignedly.

'Of course you did,' said Rameel, bowing mockingly. 'You know everything, after all.'

'I don't know everything. For example, I don't know what you're doing here,' said Azaz patiently. 'Perhaps you would care to enlighten me?'

Rameel laughed. 'Oh, I don't think so. I think it's much more fun if you find out for yourself, don't you?'

And without a backward glance he flew off.

Chapter 5

'I really think we should tell the abbess,' said Eva.

'But why?' protested Blanco.

They were walking back to the convent. After they had read what the Count had written about Blanco they no longer wanted to stay underground. They had found the string, walked back through the chambers, and climbed out of the hole. There, Eva found that the angels had disappeared, which annoyed her since they had promised to keep watch. But there was nothing she could say at the moment since they weren't there to hear it.

'Who else can we tell?'

'Why do we have to tell anyone?' he asked.

Eva stopped and put a hand on his arm. 'Blanco,' she said. 'That man has already tried to kill you once; well, tried to kill both of us, actually. And he really, really wants to try again.'

'But what could the abbess do?' asked Blanco reasonably.

That flummoxed Eva. It was true. What could she do that they couldn't do themselves?

Count Maleficio entered the church at the top of the hill, pushed aside the altarpiece to reveal a secret staircase and descended to his laboratory. He knew immediately that somebody had been there. He could sense it.

'Griffin!' he shouted.

The heap of rags which lay in the far corner of the laboratory got to its feet and shuffled over. Griffin blinked blearily at his master and rubbed the sleep from his eyes.

'Have you been here all the time?'

Griffin nodded. The Count eyed him carefully but he seemed to be telling the truth. Maybe he was imagining things. Maybe because the time was approaching when he would at last see Magdalena again, he was getting jumpy. He took the lid off the pot that was sitting on top of one of the gleaming copper furnaces and inhaled deeply.

'Almost ready,' he said.

As he replaced the lid he caught sight of his reflection in it and gave a howl of rage. The flickering candles cast an eerie glow on to the Count's face and highlighted the jagged scar that ran from his forehead to his chin. It gave a sudden painful stab as he stood there and he stroked it gently, thinking as he did so about the boy who had given it to him. Blanco Polo. Just thinking about him he felt his blood begin to churn and he had to breathe deeply to calm himself down again. He would never forgive Blanco for what he had done to his face and when he saw him again—as he was sure he would— he would make sure that the boy knew just how upset he was. Where, he wondered, was he now?

'Don't you get bored with humans?' asked Rameel with a huge yawn. He was hovering above Micha and Azaz and

had been for some time. He had appeared out of nowhere solely, it would seem, to annoy them.

'Go away, Rameel,' said Micha, looking over at Azaz. A muscle in his left wing was beginning to tug, a sure sign that he was losing his patience. She really didn't want them to start fighting.

'They're just so slow,' said Rameel. 'They take aeons to pick up the simplest ideas. Look how long it took them to make fire and develop a wheel.'

Azaz sighed.

'Come on,' he said to Micha. 'Let's go.'

'Scared are you?' taunted Rameel.

Azaz had been about to take flight, but that stopped him.

'Of what?' he asked.

'Ignore him,' said Micha.

'Have you ever wondered . . .' said Rameel in a teasing tone.

Azaz knew that he was being tempted but he couldn't resist.

'What?' he said, hovering at the very tips of his toes, his great wings trembling, ready to fly off at a moment's notice. Micha was already hovering overhead.

Rameel saw that he had him hooked, exactly as he had intended, and slowly drifted down to stand next to him. His indigo robes matched his wings and it was hard to see where one began and the other ended. His long black hair fell to his waist.

Micha sighed. A confrontation was inevitable. She knew that Rameel had always been jealous of Azaz, for Azaz had once been the leader of the rebel angels and Rameel had always coveted the position.

'I'm leaving if you two are just going to argue,' she said. 'Have you ever thought that maybe your humans are *just too stupid? I'll bet that even if you told them exactly how to do something they'd still get it wrong.'*

'Blanco wouldn't,' said Azaz. 'He's clever and quick.'

'Azaz,' said Micha warningly.

'I would wager,' continued Rameel, 'that he'll never find out what the Count is up to. I've trained the Count and I think we all know that my knowledge is far superior to yours.'

Azaz knew what Rameel was doing but he couldn't help responding.

'Whatever you get the Count to do, Blanco will do better.'

Rameel laughed, his strong teeth showing between his thin lips. 'Is that a challenge,' he jeered before flying off.

Micha looked at Azaz's furious face and sighed. 'Azaz,' she began.

He flew away from her, leaving her looking after him in dismay.

'So these men—this Count Maleficio and this man you call the Stranger—want to kill you . . . And the Count has turned up here, on Malta?'

'Actually,' said Blanco, 'it's only me they want to kill. They just want to capture Eva.'

'Because,' said Eva, looking defensive and knowing that she wouldn't be believed, 'I can talk with angels.'

The abbess did not look as surprised or horrified as she could have done. She merely lifted an eyebrow in a querying manner and motioned for Eva to proceed.

'There are two,' said Eva slowly. 'Azaz and Micha. I overheard them talking one day in the church near my home and I've been able to talk with them ever since.'

'Have you ever seen any other angels?' asked the abbess.

'Count Maleficio has an angel called Rameel helping him,' said Eva, her voice tailing away as she spoke. She suddenly realized why Azaz and Micha hadn't been at the entrance to the hole when they came back out. If the Count was here then so, in all probability, was Rameel.

'This laboratory,' said the abbess, turning her attention back to Blanco. 'What do you think it's for?'

'He's making something with firepowder,' said Blanco. 'I just don't know what he's planning to do with it.'

The abbess sat back in her seat and the light shining through the window lingered on her face. She suddenly looked much younger and her face had taken on a more lively look. Although they had found her to be infinitely kind and generous in their time at the convent they had rarely noticed her smile and had certainly never heard her laugh.

'I will have to think about this,' she said, 'before I can advise you what to do. My initial thoughts would be that you should leave the island.'

'No!' said Blanco. 'I need to know what he plans to do with the firepowder. I couldn't leave without knowing that.'

'I'm not going back to Venice,' was all Eva said.

The abbess looked at Blanco again. 'Do you really think this man is dangerous?' she asked him.

Blanco nodded. He had been about to ask her about Magdalena but with her question he realized that they had given her enough to think about for the moment. He would ask later.

'We'll let you think about what we have told you,' he said politely although, as he had commented when he talked to Eva about it, he didn't really think that there was a lot she could do. She could go to the authorities but they had no definite proof that the Count was planning to do anything with the firepowder. Of course, the fact that he was practising alchemy was a reason for taking him into custody but Blanco knew that even that was difficult to prove. Anyway, he didn't want the Count captured yet. He wanted to go back and see what he was up to. That was why he hadn't mentioned the alchemy either to Eva or to the abbess.

'Come on, Eva,' he said, getting to his feet. 'Let's give the abbess some time to think.'

Eva remained where she was. 'I need to talk to the abbess about something.'

'I think we've taken up enough of her time,' said Blanco.

'Go away, Blanco,' said Eva crossly. 'I want to speak to the abbess alone.'

Blanco looked flummoxed at this. What could Eva possibly want to say that he couldn't hear? She usually told him everything. He frowned at her but she refused to meet his eye and after a few moments he turned and left the room. He really wanted to slam the door behind him—sometimes Eva could be so infuriating—but he thought that would be rude and so didn't.

The abbess looked across the table at Eva. She saw a tall young girl with untidy, curling blonde hair and eyes and a mouth that were slightly too big for her small face. But it was a face of determination and courage, although she didn't look very brave at the moment.

'What can I do for you, my dear?' she asked kindly, although she half suspected what was coming.

'I would like you to accept me as a novice,' said Eva, staring fixedly at her hands which were clasped in her lap.

The abbess leant back in her chair and tried to pick her words carefully.

'You know, my dear,' said the abbess, 'you can't come into the convent to escape from life. It just follows you in. I should know.'

Eva glanced at her. She was tall and thin and her face seemed calm and serene but as Eva looked at her properly for the first time she saw that her eyes were filled with an almost unbearable sadness. She lowered her gaze.

'I'm not running away,' she said. 'I've always wanted to be a nun. It's just that my parents wanted to marry me off to help their business.'

The abbess had to bite back a smile at that. It was so patently untrue. And from all that she had seen or heard of Eva, anyone less suited to life within a convent was hard to imagine. But she knew that there was only one way to prove that to her.

'Very well, my dear,' she said. 'I'll give you a week's trial.'

Luca stared at the sentences, feeling the answer niggling at him in the same way as his back tooth pained him when he waggled it with his tongue. He continued to wrestle with the problem. He was almost enjoying it— it had been so long since he had been tested—but he felt a strong element of frustration as well. He had all of the letters, everything he needed, yet he couldn't find out *where* the heartstone lay. Time, he felt, was against him.

He stood up and walked over to the window. Looking down he could see the traders peddling their wares up and down the canal. The way they manoeuvred their boats round about, avoiding each other by the merest measure with a flick of a wrist, was like watching a dance.

Luca turned away from the window to survey his surroundings. He liked to be surrounded by luxury. The walls were hung with heavy red and gold tapestries. His eyes lingered on them for a moment before he turned to the painting that hung over the mantelpiece. Right in the centre of it was a young woman dressed in the brightest blue. Luca crossed the room to admire it at close quarters. The painting had cost him a small fortune because of the lady in blue. The colour came from crushed lapis lazuli stones. The heartstone was also a lapis lazuli, but a very special one, created in a particular way.

The reason the heartstone was more important than any other was because of the power that it contained. It had been created by a range of strong emotions and therefore held their energy. If that energy was released then the power would belong to the person who released it. Luca reread the legend, which the Count had found when he had solved the first code in the letters, as he tried to think of where it could possibly be.

There was a boy and a girl. They were in love. One day a fallen angel came. He saw the girl and fell in love. But she loved the boy more than the angel. The angel killed the girl and took her heart and buried it deep in the earth and covered it with a mountain and then with a coat of ice. If he could not have her heart then neither could the boy. The heartstone is deep blue with red undertones and covered with a sheer face of clear ice—like an eye filmed with tears.

Because it was created with the powerful emotions of passion, love, jealousy, and regret the heartstone contains immense power. It is believed that anyone who holds it will have the power to change one thing. But it can only be freed by someone in love—it is their tears that will free it. Where does it lie? The answer is between the lines.

But where? thought Luca, scanning the letters for the umpteenth time. Where?

Chapter 6

Eva had managed to avoid Blanco for the rest of the day but there was no escaping him the next morning. When she bumped into him she was dressed as a novice.

'Eva!' he cried. 'What are you doing dressed like that?'

'I would have thought that was perfectly obvious even to a fool like you,' she replied haughtily.

Blanco was taken aback, as much by her rudeness as by the sight of her in a novice's outfit.

'Does the abbess know?' he asked.

'Of course. She was the one who gave me the habit.'

'But . . . but . . .' He didn't quite know where to start. Did this mean that she was staying here? Not coming back to Venice? But what about the Count and the Stranger? And the angels?

'I told you I didn't want to go back to Venice,' she said.

'No, you didn't. You told me you wanted to go and then changed your mind when I said we should stay and find Magdalena!'

'But we haven't done anything about finding her,' shouted Eva. 'And I know that when you want to go you'll expect me to go with you. And. I. Don't. Want. To. Go. To. Venice!'

'You're being stupid!' he said. 'Go and tell the abbess that you've changed your mind.'

'No!' said Eva. 'How dare you tell me what to do!

You always think that you're the one in charge. Well, maybe you'll listen now!'

'What does Azaz have to say about this?'

Eva shrugged nonchalantly. 'I haven't told him yet. But it's not up to him what I do with my life.'

'This is ridiculous,' said Blanco, shaking his head and determining to go and talk to the abbess as soon as he could, to persuade her to change Eva's mind.

'At least I'm not stupid enough to moon after a novice nun,' said Eva spitefully.

Blanco looked surprised. He didn't think that anyone had noticed that he liked Sister Agatha.

'You're so annoying!' he shouted.

'Not as annoying as you!' she shouted back.

Micha and Azaz appeared and watched the argument as it escalated into a shouting match.

'What is she doing?' asked Azaz as he noticed what Eva was wearing.

Micha sighed. 'I knew we shouldn't have gone after Rameel and left her. I blame that girl.' She cast a look at the approaching Sister Agatha. 'Eva would never have done this if it hadn't been for her.'

'You know, Micha,' said Azaz, 'sometimes we can't choose who it is we like.'

Micha ignored him. She knew what she was going to do.

'Am I interrupting something?' asked a high, fluting voice and they both turned to find Sister Agatha standing behind them looking beatifically down at her toes. 'I'm sorry if I am but the abbess asked me to show Eva the daily routine.'

Eva clenched her teeth and nodded. Blanco blushed crimson, wondering if Sister Agatha had heard what Eva had shouted just a moment before.

'I hate you,' he hissed at Eva before turning and storming out of the convent gates. Sister Agatha stared after him with a small smile on her face and Eva fought to hold back her tears.

Azaz flew down and walked alongside Blanco. 'Blanco,' he said.

Blanco brushed at his neck as though something had tickled him there.

Azaz sighed. Although he had spoken to Blanco in the past, Blanco couldn't always hear him. He hadn't yet worked out how to make him hear him every time. He focused his thoughts on the hole in the ground where Blanco and Eva had found the Count's laboratory the day before.

Almost immediately Blanco changed direction.

When he had stormed off Blanco hadn't decided where he was going but he soon found that his feet were taking him in the direction of the Count's underground chambers.

He was so caught up in his fury with Eva that he was startled when something flew over his head, almost clipping his hair as it did so, and then buried itself in the earth a little way in front of him. He looked around but couldn't see anyone or anything. He moved forward a few steps. Whatever it was, it was smoking a little and he wasn't sure whether to pick it up or not. As he watched, it gave a little putter and went out and he crouched down to look at it more closely. Gingerly he pulled it. It almost broke apart but he managed to keep it all together. It was a long, thin piece of wood, hollow in the middle and charred round the edges. Things had once hung from the sides but what they were Blanco wasn't sure, for they were almost entirely burnt away. It looked a little like a long, thin bird with tiny wings. The one thing that he was sure of was that this had something to do with the Count and he wanted to know exactly what.

'Blanco,' said Azaz, who had found the miniature flying machine on the ground and had fired it over Blanco's head to get his attention.

Blanco again felt that sensation of a hot breath against his neck and suddenly it dawned on him what it was. Azaz was trying to speak to him. He concentrated hard. Eva could talk to the angels whenever she liked but Blanco could only do it occasionally and only, he suspected, when they wanted him to hear something.

'You have to tell me what the Count is doing.'

'Of course,' said Blanco and then immediately felt silly talking out loud to himself.

Arriving at the hole, Blanco took a deep breath and convinced himself that he was doing the right thing. He dropped inside and found himself completely surrounded by darkness. He had forgotten just how little light there was in the tunnel but he found that if he stood still, his eyes soon became accustomed to it and he could see the rock formations. He saw, glimmering on the floor, the string which he had dropped in his haste to escape last time. Picking it up, he began to follow it all the way to the laboratory.

The laboratory was empty. He watched and listened for a while to make sure that there really was no one there and, when he was sure, he went in.

He looked over at the table and saw the Count's notebook still lying there. He couldn't resist taking a look.

Blanco looked around the room and soon found a machine almost exactly the same as the one in the book. He looked at the notebook again.

Once the charcoal is alight, the solve-stone follows suit and when the last part of the threesome is added, the result is nothing less than spectacular. The heat from the one lights the second which engulfs the third, transforming all into a weapon of such destruction as I have previously seen only in my dreams.

I have experimented with this many times. The thunder that this beast makes is louder even than that made by God in His Heaven and almost as terrifying.

By a mixture of natural intelligence and much patience I have reached the ideal weight, size, and mixture. Now all that is needed is the final test.

When he had finished reading Blanco looked again at the object he had found outside. It was a small flying machine! There were several of them beside the Count's notebook. They were long, thin wooden tubes with small feathered wings, one on each side. They were like miniature versions of the one that Blanco had flown at the Count's castle. He inspected them from all angles. They were beautifully made. He popped one in his pocket to examine later, when he had more time. As he did so, he heard a scuffle in the corner and turned in fright, staring at where the noise had come from, terrified that at any moment the Count would appear and fulfil the threat that Blanco had read in his notebook the day before.

Instead, a silent Griffin appeared and Blanco heaved a sigh of relief. Griffin was the Count's servant but he was also the one who had helped save him and Eva back at the castle. He was utterly devoted to Eva but Blanco wasn't entirely sure that he could trust him.

'Is the Count with you?' he asked urgently, picking up another tube.

Griffin shook his head. He didn't like to speak unless he really had to. 'Eva?' he mumbled.

'She's on the island with me, but she's not here. Griffin, what is the Count doing?'

Griffin didn't answer but came over and took the wooden tube from Blanco's hands.

'Not finished,' he said, taking a small sharp knife from the table and carving a few notches in it. 'You should go. The Count could come back at any moment.'

'You made these?' said Blanco with some surprise. Griffin was so unkempt that it was easy to believe that he was clumsy and inept. As Blanco watched Griffin made some intricate carvings in the sharp front of the object. He was better than many of the master artisans that Blanco had seen in the back streets of Venice.

'But that's beautiful, Griffin,' he said. 'I had no idea that it was you who had made these.'

Griffin pushed his hood back slightly so that his face could be seen and gave a quick shy smile. Eva had told Blanco about Griffin's eyebrows, or rather the lack of them, but Blanco was still surprised by the difference that no eyebrows could make to a face. As though sensing this Griffin quickly pulled his hood forward again.

Blanco turned back to the Count's notebook and started to turn the heavy pages of parchment. Soon he was lost in them as he tried to follow the Count's experiments. He seemed to be working on more than one thing. Blanco quickly scanned the notes about the tiny flying machine on which Griffin was still working, but there were also notes on the firepowder and something which the Count called 'the beast'. These notes were to do with the illustration he had seen earlier. And then there was another section, an alchemical one. Blanco didn't know much about alchemy. It was officially frowned upon throughout Venice and the Pope had issued a proclamation only a few years before condemning it as 'an unnatural art'. But many still practised it and it had always fascinated Blanco. Now he recognized that many of the symbols in the Count's diary related to it. But it did not seem to be gold that the Count was trying to make. It was something to do with a stone made of lapis lazuli—a heartstone as he called it. Blanco knew, from his father's business, that lapis lazuli was one of the rarest and most expensive of precious stones. He was about to skip through the pages when he saw Gump's name. Puzzled, he started to read.

By the time Blanco had finished reading he was both fascinated and horrified. Once again, the Count seemed to have found a way to use firepowder in the most destructive manner possible. Now, at least, Blanco knew what the Count was planning and he knew when. What he didn't know was where.

He turned over a few more pages. Eva's name jumped out at him. He read quickly.

Rameel was sick of the Count. All he did was moan about his experiments and the island and about this stupid woman he was waiting to see, whom he hadn't seen for twenty years. Nothing was working fast enough for him and he blamed Rameel. Rameel was not happy about this since he had, in fact, told the Count what he needed to know to finish building the beast. It was just that the Count was too stupid to do it properly. That was why Rameel had taunted Azaz. Blanco, he was sure, would be able to finish the beast. Azaz would help him. He could never resist a challenge.

Rameel was delighted when he saw Azaz sitting at the mouth of the tunnel. It meant the boy was down in the laboratory, hopefully finishing the Count's experiments.

Azaz saw Rameel and the Count at the same time as Rameel saw him. He didn't know what to do. He couldn't go underground to warn Blanco. All he could do was watch as the Count walked into the church. Rameel stayed outside.

'Don't worry,' he said. 'I didn't tell him your boy was inside! I thought I'd let him find out for himself.'

Azaz glared at him. 'Blanco isn't in the church,' he said. Rameel smiled. 'No, but he is underneath it, isn't he?'

Azaz flew to the church door and looked inside. The church was empty.

They both heard it at the same time. Footfalls quickly heading their way. Griffin, who had been whittling away on another miniature flying machine as Blanco had read, clutched at Blanco's arm in terror.

'You must go,' he said. 'I won't tell him you were here.'

Blanco had never spoken much to Griffin when he had been in the Count's castle but he had little choice other than to trust him. In his haste to turn the pages back to where they had been, he knocked over a beaker with his elbow but had no time to stop and pick it up. He darted back into the little tunnel that led to the outside.

He was just in time. Once he had passed out of sight he turned back to watch. The Count's silver cloak glistened in the candlelight and he seemed to be in a foul mood.

'What have you done?' he snarled as he watched Griffin try to wipe up the substance that was dripping out of the beaker. 'You clumsy fool! I hope that's not the potion,' he continued. 'A month's work you would have lost and we're almost ready for the next stage.'

Even though he knew it was dangerous, Blanco stayed to listen.

'Come with me,' said Sister Agatha. Eva sighed heavily. Already she was beginning to think that she had made the wrong decision. Sister Agatha had had her running all over the place since Blanco had left them that morning. She felt a twinge of guilt when she thought of Blanco. She supposed that she had owed it to him to tell him what she was planning to do. But then, why should she? He had taken her to Barcelona even though she had told him that she hadn't wanted to go; he was taking her to Venice although she didn't want to go there either, and he didn't care about her anyway. She only had to think of the way that he looked at Sister Agatha compared with how he looked at her to realize that.

'Sister Penitentia!'

It took Eva a moment to realize that she was being called. She had yet to get used to her new name.

Sister Agatha was tapping her foot impatiently at the entrance to the cellar.

'Go down and fetch me some seeds,' she said. 'I'll meet you at the herb garden.'

Eva hesitated. She looked through the dark doorway. The first steps disappeared into the darkness rather quickly and it looked gloomy and forbidding. She shook her head.

'Are you refusing to do as I ask? You know that obedience is one of the most important vows of a nun,' said Sister Agatha in a mocking tone. She paused and then added, 'Won't your *angels* help you?'

Eva was filled with so much fury, at Sister Agatha, and at Blanco for daring to tell such personal things, that she was through the doorway and down the steps almost before she knew it.

'Be careful down there!' came a laughing voice as the small blot of light that had shone in from the top disappeared and Sister Agatha swung the door shut with a loud thud.

'No!' screamed Eva but she was too late. Even before the word was fully out of her mouth she was in complete darkness.

She was terrified. Enveloped in blackness, she felt as though she couldn't breathe.

'Must get out,' she sobbed to herself. 'It's only a cellar. It's only a cellar. There's nothing here.'

A sudden loud scuffling in the corner made her scream again. She fell to her hands and knees and then curled up in a ball and rocked herself backwards and forwards. She knew that she should try to find the stairs but she was too scared to move.

Micha had seen Sister Agatha shut the door and had been tempted to open it again and push Sister Agatha down to join Eva. But she resisted. She hadn't spent centuries learning patience to forget it all in an instant. However, she was surprised by the force of anger which swept over her. She flew past Sister Agatha, causing her habit to billow out. Sister Agatha look round in surprise, for it was a windless day. When she saw nothing, she continued on her way. Micha opened the cellar door for Eva and then flew after the novice.

Eva had just escaped from the cellar and turned the corner of the main building when she saw Sister Agatha. She tried to behave in a nun-like manner and not laugh too loudly but she couldn't help herself. Sister Agatha's beautiful white shift was completely covered with mud. Eva sniffed. In fact, it was covered with something much worse than mud.

'What happened to you?' she asked, trying to keep the glee from her voice.

Sister Agatha scowled. 'Nothing.'

Sister Assumpta appeared behind Sister Agatha, followed by four other nuns who all looked as though they were trying very hard not to laugh.

'Go and get yourself cleaned up, Sister Agatha,' said Sister Assumpta. 'And maybe next time you'll be more careful when you're near the middens.'

'Someone pushed me,' said Sister Agatha through gritted teeth.

'I've already told you,' said Sister Assumpta, 'that there was no one near you when you fell.'

The other nuns all nodded in agreement. Sister Agatha wasn't popular in the convent and they were delighted by what had happened.

'Someone pushed me,' repeated Sister Agatha stubbornly.

The nuns wandered away, shaking their heads either with suppressed laughter or amazement that she wouldn't accept that she had just tripped. Only Eva could see the laughing angel hovering over Sister Agatha's head.

Chapter 7

From where he sat Blanco had a perfect view. This was the first time he had seen his enemy close to since he had fled the castle in Spain weeks before. He had to bite back a shocked cry when he saw the Count's face. Ever since they had first met, one thing that had always struck Blanco was how proud the Count was of his appearance. He was never less than perfectly groomed and everything matched. He was vain. Now, however, one half of his face was puckered up by a large scar. It ran from a point on his chin, widening out along his left cheek and finishing in an untidy lump at his forehead. It looked red, sore, and angry and Blanco had the uneasy feeling that it was the result of the firecracker which he had set off in the tower room just before he and Eva jumped from the window in the flying machine.

But if the scar was angry then so was Blanco. This was a man who had befriended him, invited him to his home, and then tried to kill him. He had tried to capture Eva and, annoyed though Blanco was with Eva, he certainly didn't want her kidnapped or harmed in any way. Blanco was determined to find out what the man was up to.

'It's done,' said the Count as he walked over to the table and picked up one of the miniature flying machines. 'How many have you made?'

'Ten, master.'

'I need more. You'll have to work faster. I need them for the night after tomorrow. And I'll need the beast if I can ever get it to work.' He walked over to the large metal barrel that Blanco had been looking at earlier. He peered down the hole at the front and then pushed it. It creaked along, the big iron wheels that it rested on protesting at the weight they were being asked to carry.

'And the firepowder?' asked the Count. 'Is it ready?'

'Yes, master.'

Blanco tried desperately to think what else the Count could be doing with the firepowder. He had done a lot of experiments in Spain using the powder but most of them were to determine the make-up of it. Blanco had stolen the Count's original formula for firepowder before he left and the Count had obviously had to spend a lot of time experimenting again in order to achieve the exact mixture that he wished. Blanco suspected that some of it would be for the miniature flying machines and although he knew that they could cause some damage, he was sure that that was not all the Count was talking about. The object called 'the beast' had to have something to do with it as well.

The Count was fussing around the machine, peering at some of the levers.

'This is going to be spectacular,' he said. 'No one will ever laugh at me again. No one will ever say that Count Maleficio forgives those who wrong him. It may have taken me twenty years but this island will learn that Maleficio never forgets.'

He turned round as he spoke and the flickering candlelight caught his eyes; from where Blanco sat, they seemed to be filled with a silver fire. The Count, normally so restrained, seemed to have become much more emotional than Blanco remembered. Blanco shrank back against the wall, even though he knew he couldn't be seen.

'Is the potion ready?' the Count demanded.

Griffin shook his head. 'Almost, master, almost. It has not boiled for long enough.' He paused. 'Do you think it will work, master?'

A flicker of doubt crossed the Count's face.

'It must work,' he said.

'Have you seen her?' asked Griffin.

'From a distance,' said the Count. 'I don't wish to speak to her without the potion. It is too much to risk.'

'Has she changed much, master?'

'It has been twenty years, you fool,' sneered the Count. Then his voice softened. 'But actually, no, she hasn't changed that much. She is still as beautiful now as she was then.'

Two things struck Blanco at the same time. Firstly, that Griffin was speaking in an abnormally loud voice and was undoubtedly doing so for his benefit and, secondly, that they had to be talking about Magdalena. So she was still here on the island and the Count had seen her. But what was this potion that he was speaking of? Was it one of the love potions that Eva had told him about? Surely he wasn't planning to give her one of those? Blanco mused on this for a moment but his attention was soon diverted when he heard his own name mentioned.

'That boy,' said the Count. 'Blanco.'

Griffin jumped.

'He's here.'

Blanco leapt to his feet ready to run.

'Here on this island.'

Blanco didn't dare to breathe lest he make a sound, even as he wondered how the Count could possibly know that he was on the island.

'I will find him,' said the Count. 'And when I do, I shall kill him. He has ruined my looks.' He stroked the left side of his face, almost caressing the scar that marked it.

The cold, definite tones of the Count left Blanco in no doubt that he meant what he said and that Blanco would do well to stay out of his way.

'And if the girl is with him,' continued the Count, 'I shall take her with me to Venice and Señor Ferron will finally have to agree that I am more useful than he would care to admit.'

Was that the Stranger's name then? Blanco wondered. They had found a scrap of paper bearing the writing 'Luca Ferr . . .' after the castle had burnt down. The Stranger must be Luca Ferron. So Eva had been right when she said that she didn't want to go back to Venice. He was there waiting for her. Or was Luca Ferron yet another person? Blanco shook his head in confusion.

He decided that he had heard enough and started to creep away. Unfortunately he tripped on one of the rocks that lay scattered about on the ground, kicking it hard enough to make it ricochet off the wall. The sound was loud in the now quiet chamber, for the Count was peering into the furnace and Griffin was in the corner whittling one of his flying machines.

'Who's there?' demanded the Count, swinging round, his silver-grey cloak whirling out behind him as he did so. It nearly got caught in the flames but he snatched it out of the way just in time.

Before Blanco knew it, the Count was clutching the back of his tunic and pulling him into the room. 'You!'

Blanco was terrified. The last time he had seen the Count, the Count had tried to kill him, and he had just heard him say that he wanted to try again. Desperation gave him strength and he fought back.

'Let go of me!' he shouted as he stamped as hard as he could on the Count's foot. Unfortunately the soft leather shoes that he wore made little impact. The pair danced around the chamber in a macabre duet as Blanco tried to loosen the Count's hold.

'I'm going to kill you!' hissed the Count. 'Look what you did to my face!'

'You were trying to murder me!'

Blanco was petrified. The Count was so much stronger and taller than he was and had his arm in such a grip it was hard to move. He saw one chance and pretended to fall forward, pulling the Count a little way with him. He then threw himself backwards into the Count, causing him to stumble. In an instant the silver cloak was caught in the furnace which lay to his left. The Count let go of Blanco to save it and in the process knocked off the pot which lay on the top.

'Look what you have done to my cloak!' he roared as three small but perfectly formed circles burnt their way through the silver material. Then he realized what he had knocked over.

'My love potion!' he howled as it spread across the floor. He dropped to his knees trying to scoop it up. It was dark red in colour and as it surrounded the Count it looked as though he knelt in a pool of blood.

He stared up at Blanco and if Blanco had thought he was furious before it was as nothing to how he was now. Blanco, still on his feet, took the opportunity he was given and turned and fled.

In Venice, Luca Ferron had finally had a stroke of luck. By accident he had left some of the stolen letters on an open windowsill in his apartment, where they had got wet in the rain. When he retrieved them, he saw that the original ink had dissolved but in between every line lay more lines of writing. His joy was great when he first saw them, thinking they would hold the key to the location of the lapis lazuli heartstone. That joy was diminished slightly when he started to read. It was the private correspondence between Marco and Magdalena. Nonetheless it made for very interesting reading, even if only to find out about a young Count Maleficio.

Marco, my only one, read the first letter, *it is painful not to see you any more. When I think back on the days and hours that we spent together when we first met, it pains my heart that we can now see each other so little.*

Luca skipped down a few lines, which were full of more drivel, to where the name Christobal caught his eye. He knew that was Maleficio's real name.

Christobal is there, wherever I am. He never seems to leave me alone and because he has my father's blessing, I cannot tell him to leave me be. He just stares at me with adoring eyes which send shivers of unease down my spine.

Luca could not stop a spiteful smile from playing about his lips. The way that Maleficio always spoke about Magdalena, it was as though she had really liked him but happened to prefer Marco Polo. Reading these letters it soon became obvious that she had never thought much of him. He read on until he came to one in another hand—obviously Marco's.

The plans are laid for this very night. I have done as you asked and have found a ship for us to set sail on. There will be a priest waiting for us before we board so that we can be married . . .

There were quite a few more practical details, as well as some declarations of love, which Luca skimmed over. He sat back and looked at the letters which he had spread out on the table in front of him. Marco and Magdalena had obviously laid extensive plans to elope and yet they had never come to fruition. What had happened to prevent them? He had little doubt that Maleficio had something to do with it, but what?

Marriage, he suddenly thought, would be a wonderful way to get what he wanted. There was no reason in the world why he shouldn't make an offer for the lovely Eva di Montini. Her family, he was sure, would be delighted to accept. He was, after all, eminently eligible, being extremely rich. The fact that he was older by some forty years he knew would not bother them for they had initially planned to marry her off to a man of his age. And her value could only have decreased since she had been gallivanting around the place with a boy, completely unchaperoned, and had left her previous fiancé at the church door. He might even apprise them of the fact that he was aware of her angels and they didn't bother him in the slightest. He sat back and smiled, his whole face changing with the look. Marriage was definitely the answer. Now all he had to do was wait for her to return to Venice.

He carried on reading, at first scared to believe what he saw but then with increasing excitement as he realized that the location of the heartstone was finally being revealed to him.

Chapter 8

When Blanco heard what had happened to Sister Agatha he blamed Eva. Of course, Sister Agatha hadn't told him outright. She had hummed and hawed when he had found her crying, saying that she didn't want to tell tales about his friends.

'I was nowhere near her,' said Eva. 'You can ask anyone. I had just heard all the noise and come round the corner.'

Blanco thought she was looking a little too pleased with herself. 'It didn't have to be you who did the pushing,' he said.

Eva didn't reply.

'How dare you interfere?' shouted Azaz.

'It was just a bit of fun,' laughed Micha. 'She had locked Eva in the cellar and I thought it served her right.'

Azaz frowned. 'It doesn't do to meddle,' he said. 'Look at Blanco and Eva arguing. You haven't helped at all.'

Micha glanced over at Eva, who quickly glanced away, pretending that she hadn't been listening.

Micha leaned forward and spoke quietly in Azaz's ear. 'How dare you tell me not to interfere,' she said. 'With your history.'

Azaz was annoyed. He was longing to help Blanco finish the Count's invention and wipe that smug grin off Rameel's face, but so far he was restraining himself. Blanco had told him about the beast and he knew he could make it work. But he also knew that it was wrong and so he had told Blanco nothing. Now he started to ask himself why he should bother trying to do the right thing when he was getting accused of interfering anyway.

'Just remember,' he said, looking Micha straight in the eye, 'if anything happens, it was you who started it.'

'Are you listening to me?' demanded Blanco.

Eva had been but with only one ear. The other one was listening to the angels.

'Of course,' she said, a bit annoyed because it had just been getting interesting on the angel side.

'Now,' he said, trying to sound patient and understanding. 'When are you going to give up this ridiculous idea of being a nun?'

Eva had actually tired of it rather quickly and was hoping to have a word with the abbess later but at Blanco's words she straightened her back. 'It's not a ridiculous idea,' she said. 'It's what I want to do. And there's nothing you can do to stop me.'

'Oh really?' said Blanco, taking a threatening step towards her. 'When I get back to Venice I could tell your father where you are. He'd soon put a stop to it.'

'You wouldn't!' said Eva in horror.

'I might.'

Eva stared at him, trying to work out if he was being serious.

'Where have you been all day?' she suddenly asked him.

It was his turn to look discomfited. 'Nowhere.' He wasn't sure why he didn't want to admit to Eva that not only had he been back to the chamber but that he had also had a fight with the Count.

'I hope you haven't been back to the chamber,' she said suspiciously. She became aware that the angels had stopped talking.

'I don't understand why you want to stay as a nun on this island when the Count lives here,' said Blanco, finding a way to avoid the question.

Eva hadn't thought of that.

'I'm sure he won't stay for long,' she said.

'He might if he finds Magdalena.'

'But she didn't love him. She'll send him away.'

'We don't know that,' replied Blanco, 'and anyway he has all those love potions.'

Eva frowned at him. 'You always try to ruin everything I do,' she said, turning to walk away.

'Where are you going?'

'To prayers and then bed. I'm a nun. I have to be obedient.'

Blanco watched Eva's retreating back with a small smile and wondered just how long her obedience would last. Then he started thinking about what he had read in the Count's notebook about her.

'Where are you going?'

Eva looked round, startled by the question. She was unused to having her every move watched. She squinted into the morning sun as she turned to face her questioner.

Sister Agatha stood there with an unpleasant look on her face.

'I don't think that's any of your business,' she answered sharply.

'Everything is everyone's business in here,' said Sister Agatha. 'You're supposed to be in seclusion. If you're going to stay here then you must follow the rules.'

'Well, maybe I don't want to stay here,' replied Eva.

'Blanco says that he wants to stay for a while,' said Sister Agatha with a smug little smile.

'Blanco can do what he likes. We don't have to do the same thing.' Eva leaned towards Sister Agatha and sniffed slightly. Sister Agatha blushed and backed away a little. She had scrubbed her garments over and over the night before but she was sure that there was still a lingering smell.

'He's lovely, isn't he?' said Sister Agatha shooting a sly look Eva's way. 'I think he likes me.'

'He's not lovely,' replied Eva shortly. 'He's horrible and rude and he never ever listens. I wouldn't believe a word he says if I were you.'

She stormed through the convent gate, ignoring the gaping-mouthed novice.

Blanco was trying to persuade himself that he really shouldn't go back to the Count's laboratory because it was far too dangerous. After all, he had been lucky to escape yesterday. But something was driving him on, something akin to what he had felt about the flying machine. He had thought of the beast and what the Count had written in his notebook all night and he had a tiny inkling of how he could make it work.

He was still thinking of this when he suddenly saw the Count in the distance, near the church. He was bending over something and as Blanco watched he stretched up and then kicked it. Then he pulled up a few bushes and tried to hide what he was working on before leaving again. Straightaway Blanco guessed what it was and knew he couldn't resist going to have a look.

Eva was completely lost. She had started heading in what she was sure was the right direction for the Count's laboratory but she very quickly lost her bearings. She ended up at the coast long before she had seen anything she recognized. She decided that she might as well go and dip her feet in the water for a while. She was so hot. Having made up her mind, she scrambled down a small cliff to the rocky shore. There she took off her sandals and carried them, splashing along in the water. The water felt so cool on her hot dusty feet and she could almost ignore the sun beating down on her head if her feet were cool.

But she soon came across a cliff that was impossible to climb. The waves crashing against the bottom of it looked far too strong for her even to begin to contemplate swimming round to the next cove, which she could, frustratingly, see. There was no help for it, she decided. She would have to retrace her steps. She turned round, only to find two of the largest men she had ever seen blocking her path. And if that weren't bad enough, they had swords in their hands. Swords which looked as if they had been used many times before.

* * *

Standing in the grass was what the Count had referred to in his notes as 'the beast'. It was the invention with which he was having so much bother because he couldn't get it to work properly. Blanco couldn't help but admire it, even though he knew that it must be totally destructive. The thing was, he knew what to do to make it work. He could tell by looking that the Count just had some of the balances wrong. Almost without meaning to, he reached out and touched the machine. At the same time a warm wind blew against his neck. He withdrew his hand quickly.

'I wasn't going to do anything,' he said guiltily.

Azaz had been wrestling with himself. He knew he couldn't interfere but he did so hate to see an invention going wrong, especially when it was so easy to fix. And it meant that he could prove to Rameel that Blanco was better than the Count and thus that he, Azaz, was better than Rameel. And, after all, Micha had interfered and nothing much had happened. What harm could it do?

In their excitement, what neither Blanco nor Azaz noticed was that they were being watched.

Scared, Eva forced herself to look around the cabin. It was surprisingly well furnished. It looked very different from the basic, wooden cabins she had been in before. This one was opulent. The double bunk was swathed in red velvet and there was even a highly polished desk and chair. On top of a dresser, which was nailed to the floor, was a silver brush, comb, and mirror set. Somehow she couldn't think that any of the sailors that she had met would have much use for anything of the sort. Unfortunately she could think of a very vain Count and Stranger who would be happy using them.

The two men who had brought her to the ship hadn't said a word to her. She was unsure if it was because they had been forbidden, because they didn't speak her language, or because they couldn't speak at all. She had known that it would be pointless to try to run away. They could both have outrun her easily and, anyway, they had those swords—the points of which Eva had no inclination to feel. Along with her fear, a heavy sense of inevitability and resignation swept over her. The Stranger had managed to capture her after all. All she could do now was wait for him to appear. She sank down on the bed and shut her eyes. What must Blanco be thinking? she wondered. She heard the door open but she refused to open her eyes.

'Just a little bit more,' said Blanco, his fingers working feverishly at one of the levers on the machine.

'To the left,' said Azaz.

Blanco heard the voice and wondered, as always, whether he really was hearing an angel's voice or whether he had just been travelling with Eva for too long. He was grateful for the help, however, for he knew he would never have managed so quickly otherwise. He pushed the lever gently to the left and then sat back on his heels.

'I think that'll work.' The components of firepowder were lying tantalizingly close, just underground. It would be amazing to see it go off, especially as there was no one around who could get hurt. He couldn't resist . . .

* * *

'Aunt Hildegard!'

Standing in front of Eva, looking remarkably similar to the last time she had seen her, was her aunt. Tall, thin, frowning, although her hair was pulled less tightly from her forehead and she was no longer dressed in grey and brown but in a simple, blue, beautifully cut gown. Eva was astounded. Her aunt had been on the ship on which they had originally left Venice. When it had been attacked by pirates her aunt had chosen to stay behind and had entrusted Eva into Blanco's hands.

'Eva!' said her aunt, in the same disgusted tone that she had always used with her. 'What have you been doing?'

She stepped forward and, with a corner of her dress, started to wipe Eva's face, which was covered in dirt.

'I can see that you are no more ladylike than you were the last time I saw you.'

Eva stilled her aunt's hand and then surprised them both by giving her a big hug. Aunt Hildegard hesitated for a moment and then returned it.

'I thought you were dead,' exclaimed Eva when they finally released each other and sat down on the bed.

'Didn't Blanco tell you that he had met me?'

'Well, yes, he did,' admitted Eva, 'but I thought he was just telling me that to cheer me up. We'd just had a very bad experience.'

'With Señor Massana?'

Eva nodded, suddenly realizing just how much she had to tell her aunt about all she had done since she had last seen her. But first she had to ask her something.

'Aunt Hildegard,' she said seriously, taking one of her aunt's hands in both of hers. 'You have to tell me. Have you been forced to stay on this ship?'

Once again her aunt astonished her, this time by

throwing her head back and laughing. Eva gazed at her in wonder. Never in her fourteen years had she seen her aunt laugh. It completely transformed her face.

'No, my dear,' said Aunt Hildegard. 'Not at all.' She looked round. 'Where is Blanco? Why isn't he with you?'

Eva frowned and looked down, pleating the material of her habit between her fingers.

'We had a fight,' she admitted. 'He kept talking to this other girl and ignoring me and then when I became a nun he got really angry and . . .'

'You're a nun?' asked Aunt Hildegard in disbelief.

'Well, probably not now,' admitted Eva.

There was a knock at the door.

'Enter!' called Aunt Hildegard.

A large bulk with its head down shuffled in. He was carrying a tray with a decanter and two glasses on it which he put down on a little table screwed to the wall.

'Thank you, Snouty,' said Aunt Hildegard. 'That will be all.'

Snouty smiled at her. They had all moaned when the captain had first brought a woman aboard, believing that she could only bring them bad luck, but the opposite had proved to be the case. They had never had so much success as in the past few months. She was a little bit fussy about killing and captives and all that, but still, she had proved to be lucky for them.

His smile faded however as he saw who she was with. His eyes still smarted in bright sunlight. 'What're you doing here?' he growled.

Eva had recognized him instantly and had shrunk back against her aunt.

'Snouty!' snapped Aunt Hildegard. 'Mind your manners. This is my niece, Eva.'

Snouty's face changed. If she was related to the captain's woman then that might mean that she was lucky too.

'Sorry,' he said gruffly but sincerely. 'And for the other day too.'

'What?' asked Aunt Hildegard. 'What happened the other day?'

'Oh, nothing,' said Eva airily as she saw Snouty looking at her pleadingly. 'I ran into . . . erm . . . Snouty and he couldn't tell me where I was.'

'Hmm,' said Aunt Hildegard, looking between the pair of them suspiciously, but they both looked back at her with big innocent eyes. 'Very well, Snouty, you may go.'

As the door closed behind him she turned back to her niece. 'Well, Eva,' she said. 'You had better tell me exactly what is going on.'

Chapter 9

Blanco slowly wiped the oil off his hands and stood back from the beast. 'Are you sure this is right?' he said. 'I don't want to get my fingers blown off.'

There was no reply but he assumed that Azaz would stop him if he was doing something wrong.

'*He's coming back.*'

'Who?' asked Blanco impatiently, completely engrossed in the beast.

'*The Count, of course.*'

'What shall I do?'

'*You have to destroy it,*' said Azaz. '*We should never have completed it.*'

'Destroy it?' Blanco's voice came out as a high squeak. 'I've only just made it work!'

As he spoke, he looked up, trying to get a glimpse of Azaz. As always, the most he got was a quivering red light, such as he also got when he looked at the sun for too long.

'I won't,' he said, standing up and crossing his arms mutinously over his chest. Once standing he saw that the Count was indeed approaching. By some odd miracle he was walking backwards and so hadn't seen him. Blanco quickly camouflaged the cannon again.

'*Too late,*' said Azaz. '*You must hide.*' He was beginning to regret having got involved. Now that he knew the

invention would work the initial excitement had dis-
appeared. He shouldn't have helped Blanco. But maybe he
would have a chance to destroy it.

The Count was walking backwards because he was
watching the men he had hired from the village. They
had fallen behind and he was urging them to hurry up.
When he turned and looked at where he knew the beast
was hidden, he cursed aloud with frustration. He had
been trying all morning to get it to work and to ignore
Rameel's taunts because he couldn't. He really needed
it for tonight. Although, if Magdalena was nice to him
this afternoon then he might decide not to test it on
Mdina—and risk blowing the whole island up.

'She won't get away this time.'

Blanco, hiding behind some bushes, heard those
words and thought that the Count could only be talking
about Eva. He had dashed into the church and then
come out clutching a vial of liquid and muttering. Even
worse, while he had been in there, the men from the
village had arrived and were now standing around
uncertainly. The Count addressed them.

'I want you to stay here,' he said firmly. 'You must
guard this and do not let anyone enter the church.'

The men shuffled their feet and nodded. They didn't
think anyone would want to go down into the church—
everyone round here knew it was haunted. And they
couldn't see that anyone would be interested in a metal
and wooden contraption. But they were being well paid
and so they would happily guard them if that was what
the man in the silly silver cloak wanted them to do.

'Wait a minute,' said the Count and crouched down

next to the beast. Something had changed. He hadn't left it like this. As he looked he couldn't stop a huge smile from crossing his face. He had brought the men to protect everything because he was worried that Blanco might try to ruin all his work now that he knew what it was. What he hadn't expected was what must have happened: Blanco had come back and finished the invention for him. He laughed out loud and started to stride away.

Blanco was torn. He needed to destroy the machine but he had to stop the Count from finding Eva.

'Go,' said Azaz. 'I'll destroy the machine.'

Rameel smiled. This was all going exactly according to plan.

Blanco had had a lot of problems staying hidden as he followed the Count. There were not many hiding places on the way and the Count kept turning round, almost as if he knew he was being followed. Blanco had to keep ducking down behind small bushes and shrubs and he wasn't very happy. It took him a while to realize that he knew the route that the Count was following. He was heading straight for the convent. Who could have told him that that was where he and Eva were staying?

Eva was looking forward to telling Blanco about Aunt Hildegard and set about trying to find him as soon as she arrived back at the convent. It was just bad luck that the first person she ran into was Sister Agatha.

'Where have you been?' Sister Agatha demanded, hands on hips and scowling. 'I've had to do all your chores because you couldn't be found.'

Eva ignored her question and asked one of her own. 'Have you seen Blanco?'

Sister Agatha had just opened her mouth to reply

when Eva surprised her by turning and running into the chapel.

Blanco had lost sight of the Count once he entered the convent grounds. He had been stopped at the gate by one of the nuns who had asked him some ridiculously long question about Venice. By the time he got in, the Count was gone.

Azaz and Rameel stared at each other and then a large smile spread across Rameel's face.

'Thank you,' he said, 'for making my task so much easier.'

Azaz scowled but couldn't say anything in return. He knew he had been a fool. He should have seen all along that Rameel was trying to trick him into getting Blanco to do what the Count could not.

He flew up into the air and then darted down towards the beast but he wasn't quite quick enough. Rameel flew straight into him, his head ramming into Azaz's chest and winding him. He was much stronger than the last time they had fought at the Count's castle. Azaz bounced on the air currents and decided that he was not going to be able to destroy the beast by fighting Rameel. He would have to find another way. He flew off, trying to ignore the sound of Rameel's mocking laughter.

Blanco found Eva in the chapel and thought that he had never been so glad to see anyone, although he didn't tell her that. Instead he shouted at her for disappearing.

'Blanco, you'll never guess who's just arrived at the convent,' interrupted Eva when she finally got a chance.

'The Count,' said Blanco. 'I know. I followed him here.'

'Does that mean that you were at the chambers again?'

'Where did he go?' he said, ignoring her last comment.

'That's the worrying thing,' said Eva. 'He went straight into the abbess's room. He didn't even knock and she didn't look surprised to see him. I could see her through the open door.'

Blanco sank down slowly on a pew. He knew from what he had heard the day before that the Count had known that Blanco was on the island before the Count had actually seen him. So someone must have told him and it would seem that that someone was the abbess.

'But she knows everything about us,' he whispered.

'Not everything,' said Eva smugly. 'She doesn't know that my Aunt Hildegard is docked in the next bay and is willing to take us anywhere we want to go!'

'*What?*'

Eva nodded excitedly. 'Don't you see?' she said. 'We don't have to stay here and we don't have to go to Venice. We can go wherever we want.'

Blanco said nothing for a moment. Then, 'I need to stay here.'

Eva frowned. 'Because of Sister Agatha?'

Blanco looked surprised. 'No,' he said, 'because the Count is planning something and I think I know how to stop him. But I think you should go.'

'I'm not going without you,' she said, hurt that he would even suggest it.

Blanco hesitated. He didn't want to tell her what was written in the Count's notes about her but he knew that she was in danger. If she went off with her aunt then she might be safe. She certainly wouldn't be safe if the Count managed to capture her.

'Don't be stupid,' he said.

She shook her head stubbornly and Blanco knew that there was only one way to make her go.

'I don't want you here,' he said. 'You'll just get in the way, like you always do. You've already caused trouble between Sister Agatha and me and I want to ask her father if I can marry her.'

Eva looked as though he had slapped her. She gazed at him in disbelief.

'No!' she breathed out.

Blanco nodded his head vigorously and then leaned forward. 'Just go,' he said. 'Your aunt gave you into my charge all those months ago. Well, now she can take the responsibility back. I've done my part.'

Micha caught up with Eva as she ran.

'Where are you going?' she asked.

'Away.' She could barely see where she was going for the tears streaming down her cheeks.

'Where's Blanco?'

Eva stopped running. 'I don't care,' she said, 'and I don't care if I never see him again. I'm going back to my aunt. He can stay here with that stupid, simpering Sister Agatha. I don't care.'

'Eva, wait!' called Micha. She knew that Eva wouldn't be safe if she were separated from Blanco.

But Eva didn't listen. She just ran on.

★　★　★

90

Azaz managed to catch Blanco's attention as he came running out of the convent.

'Did you destroy it?' asked Blanco.

Azaz had to admit to his failure.

The boy and the angel stood side by side, each gnawing on their lips.

'What,' asked Blanco, 'are we going to do now?'

Chapter 10

Blanco was lying in the tall grass, trying to see exactly what it was that the Count was doing. He had made the men wheel the beast closer to the town and now they were ferrying barrels and other things from the underground chamber. The Count had brought even more men back from the town with him and Blanco had no idea how he could possibly get near enough to the beast to dismantle it. He had thought of confronting the abbess to see what she knew but had decided that that would just waste time. He had a feeling that whatever the Count had prepared, it was imminent. At least, he thought, Eva was safe. She would be off the island and on board Aunt Hildegard's ship by now.

The Count could barely contain his excitement. This was so much better than the flying machine that he and Blanco had built together. For one thing he could play a full part in this whereas he had had to leave the piloting of the flying machine to Blanco, because of his fear of heights. He cursed. He shouldn't have thought of the boy. Every time he thought of him his blood began to boil. He stroked his scar. He couldn't believe that the lad had escaped again. He would kill him tomorrow before he sailed to Venice. He would kill

Blanco and take the girl. And, with the girl, he would get the lapis lazuli heartstone and claim the power that it held.

'Master,' said Griffin. 'It is time.'

The Count rubbed his hands together. He loved this part. He looked up. Griffin was holding a flaming torch and in its light he could see the men standing around him, with varying looks of wonder or stupidity in their eyes. They were fools, every one of them. They had left their homes and would watch as their town went up in flames. The Count shook his head. He would never cease to be amazed by the stupidity of some people; by the fact that some people would do anything for a handful of coins.

Blanco decided that he had to try to get to the beast, even if he was caught. He crept forward. There was no one actually standing over it and he knew that if he could just pull out one of the levers then it wouldn't work. He started to crawl.

The Count had turned round to look at the walls of Mdina which towered above them only a short distance away. He had been planning this since he had arrived on the island about a month before. He needed to try the miniature flying machines and the beast somewhere and on Malta he could make his escape before anyone had even worked out what was going on. Nobody knew he was here except Magdalena and that brat Blanco, who would die anyway. As for Magdalena, if she had loved him he might not have attempted it. But she had laughed at him and made fun of him and told him that she could never love him. His blood began to boil more vigorously at the thought. Everybody he had ever loved or befriended had betrayed him. But now they would see what he could do! And if she blew up with the town, so much the better. She meant nothing to him now anyway.

Griffin had already prepared the charcoal and sulphur and all they had to do was add the solve-stone. These were the little white crystals which Eva had thought so pretty when she saw them in the Count's laboratory. They were deadly little ornaments, however, for when combined with the charcoal and sulphur and then lit they caused the mixture to explode. What the Count had done was really rather ingenious. Through his various experiments, he had worked out that if he mixed the powders in a certain way then the little flying machines would fly forward before exploding, using the power of the firepowder. He had lined up five of them. They wouldn't do a great deal of damage to the town since most of it was built of stone but there was the odd wooden roof which might be set alight. And then there was the beast! If the Count's calculation was correct, the bronze ball that would go flying out of it would cause tremendous damage. He had aimed it straight at the convent.

Nothing was going to stop him.

Eva had stopped crying by the time Azaz reached her. Instead she was mad, hopping mad, at the way that Blanco had treated her.

'Go away, Azaz,' she snapped when Azaz appeared and immediately launched into a story of how Blanco was in trouble. 'Blanco can look after himself. He made it perfectly clear that he doesn't need me.'

'What have you done, Azaz?' asked Micha. She knew

from the look on his face that he was as deeply involved as Blanco.

'I—' He stopped, knowing that Micha was going to be furious with him. Then he continued, 'I'll tell you later. It's to do with the firepowder.'

Eva shrugged. 'I don't know anything about it,' she said. 'I just don't understand the fascination. And what does it matter anyway? What harm can it do?'

'The Count has aimed his machine straight at the convent. He could cause a lot of damage.'

Eva shrugged again.

'Remember the church in the Count's village in Spain?' asked Azaz.

Eva nodded. After the Count had used the firepowder there, there had been no church. There had, instead, been only a large hole in the ground where the church should have been. But Blanco had sent her away. He could just deal with it himself. After all, what could she do?

Blanco had just put out a hand to tug on one of the levers when he was hauled to his feet. Cursing, he fought with the man who had grabbed him but he was held in too strong a grip. The man started to shout, attracting everyone's attention, including the Count's.

The angels had flown off after trying to persuade Eva to come with them. They were determined to do what they could. Eva walked out on the deck of her aunt's ship. She leant on the rail and looked at the cliff which lay before her. She barely noticed as her aunt came to stand beside her.

'You never told me why Blanco didn't come with you.'

'He sent me away.' Eva moved her gaze from the cliff to the bright blue sea and watched as the waves crashed upon each other. 'He said he was going to marry Sister Agatha.'

Aunt Hildegard peered at her niece.

'I may not have liked that young man when I first met him,' she said, 'but it seems to me that he has proved himself over and over again in the adventures that you have had and I can't believe that he would just send you away like that. He must have had his reasons.'

'Azaz says . . .' began Eva.

Aunt Hildegard sighed. 'I will accept many things from you, my dear, but I won't accept that you can talk to angels. Perhaps you would like to rephrase?'

'I suppose Blanco might have sent me away because I'm in danger. You remember that mad Count that I told you about? The one with the flying machine? Well, he's here and I think he's going to do something dreadful and Blanco has gone to stop him. Maybe I should go and help but I don't know what I can do alone.'

Aunt Hildegard laughed. 'I think I know someone who can help you.'

The Count was delighted. Things were going completely to plan, even better than planned, in fact, for in addition to testing out the beast and the miniature flying machines he had managed to capture Blanco. He glared over at where Blanco lay, firmly bound. Blanco glared back. The Count allowed himself to smile. It really couldn't be any better.

The first hint that things might not be going according to his plans was when Rameel spoke.

'There are people coming,' he said.

The Count jumped. He couldn't see Rameel, he could only hear him, and so he was constantly taken by surprise by him—something that Rameel had infinite fun with.

'Who?' he asked.

Rameel was unable to answer. Suddenly his mouth was held shut by a pair of strong arms and he was being carried away. His legs and wings were trapped. He could struggle, he knew, but he also knew there was no point. And there was nothing that could be done to prevent things now. He relaxed and enjoyed the feel of the night air against his face as Micha and Azaz carried him away.

When Rameel said nothing more, the Count persuaded himself that he had just imagined hearing his voice. The first miniature flying machine was ready. The machines were placed on a wooden frame. The Count stood back and took a light from the flaming torch that Griffin held. The men watched open-mouthed as he touched it to the smaller end of the first flying machine and the spark entered the tiny chamber of the wooden object. It then shuddered forward, the wings on the side of it flapping wildly. Their mouths opened even wider when it took flight. It shot past in a blaze of orange glory, lighting the darkness so that it was almost as bright as daylight.

The Count was delighted and watched as it sped towards the walls. It went even faster than he had anticipated and in the growing darkness its light was highly visible. It looked like a star falling from the sky. But when it reached the walls, it exploded with a loud crash and some of the men shouted with horror.

The Count turned round to grin in triumph at Griffin and to get him to light the others. Griffin wasn't paying attention and so the Count grabbed the lit torch from his hand and placed it against the ends of two more of the miniature flying machines.

The men gasped as the machines took off. Some of them turned to flee, so convinced were they that they were watching the work of demons. The Count laughed. He had underestimated just how terrified they would be. He was so used to seeing the machines that he had forgotten how unusual they were. He looked towards the walls of the town and laughed even louder when he saw that the rockets were indeed hitting their targets. In the quiet of the night the Count could hear screams coming from inside the walls. He looked round at Griffin who was staring open mouthed, not at where the miniature flying machines were, but off to the left. As the Count lifted his blazing torch he saw why. There were about twenty pirates grinning down at him.

That was all he had time to see before there was mayhem. The few townsmen who had remained turned to fight the pirates, whom they hated because of the trouble they caused on the island. Within moments a full-scale fight had broken out. The frame holding the flying machines was smashed and they were being trampled on.

'Be careful!' cried the Count as a heavy-footed pirate crushed one of the machines completely.

'They were a good idea, Count,' said a voice from behind him. 'But then your ideas are always good. It's what you do with them that's bad.'

The Count turned in a furious rage, ignited by that smug voice. He hated that voice and he hated its owner. He ruined everything. He ruined all his experiments and he had ruined his looks. With a roar of anger he leapt on Blanco, who had been unbound by one of the pirates. Blanco felt the Count's fingers wrapping themselves round his neck. He could smell the sulphur on the Count's hands. Everything seemed to be happening very slowly and very clearly. He could feel every stone on the ground under his back.

I don't want to die, he thought and tried to fight back. But the Count was immensely strong and although Blanco could see that Eva had appeared from somewhere and was pummelling the Count's back, she seemed to be making no difference. None of the pirates had noticed. Everything began to go a little dark around the edges. Was this the end?

'Christobal!'

A woman's voice, sharp and cross, cut into his thoughts. Who was Christobal?

'Christobal! Let him go!'

The Count's fingers were loosening. Blanco drew in a deep, ragged breath, feeling his throat burn as he did so. He pushed the Count off and crawled away from him.

The Count got slowly to his feet and turned to face the abbess.

'Magdalena,' he said. 'What are you doing here?'

Magdalena? Blanco and Eva exchanged shocked glances but said nothing.

'Why are you trying to kill that boy?'

'Why does it matter?' demanded Eva angrily. 'You were going to hand us over anyway!'

Blanco looked at the city walls. There were fires breaking out all over Mdina, although none of them was large as yet.

'What?' queried the abbess, looking puzzled. 'Why would I have done that? Until yesterday I hadn't seen him for twenty years!'

'But you never said you knew him when we talked about the flying machines,' said Eva, unwilling to give up. 'We mentioned his name then.'

'You mentioned a Count Maleficio,' said the abbess and then her voice tailed away as she turned to face the Count. 'What have you been saying, Christobal?'

The Count grimaced in the flickering light of the torches which surrounded them.

'He's not a count,' she said, turning back to Eva and Blanco. 'His name is Christobal Vellatin. That was why I said I didn't know him. I never knew him by the name Maleficio.'

'But someone told him we were here,' said Blanco, looking confused. 'If it wasn't you, then who was it?'

'Me,' said another voice, just audible above the fighting pirates and townsmen.

'Why, what a gathering we have now,' said the Count sarcastically. 'This wasn't meant to be a party.'

Blanco stared at the newcomer in disbelief.

'I'm sorry, Blanco,' said Sister Agatha, shrugging her shoulders in what he had once thought was a pretty way. 'I needed the money.'

'But you live in a convent,' said Blanco. 'Why would you need money?'

'Because I don't want to live in a convent,' she replied sadly. 'I need money for my dowry and he was going to give it to me.'

The abbess interrupted her. 'You certainly won't be staying in my convent any longer,' she said.

'Actually,' said the Count spitefully, 'it's my convent.'

'What?' said the abbess.

'Yes,' he said. 'I endowed that convent for you. It's me you have to thank for that. If it hadn't been for me you'd have been thrown out by your father with nowhere to go. After all that business with Marco and those letters; after I'd told you he'd died and you were so distraught; after you'd turned me down for the fourth time; after that I still wanted to look after you and so I had this convent built for you. *I loved you!*'

This last came out as a howl.

'Well, I didn't ask you to do any of those things!' shouted the abbess. 'I loved Marco and I never wanted to be a nun! If Marco hadn't died then you wouldn't have had to build the convent because I would have married him, so don't pretend it was some great act of generosity!'

The Count was aghast at her dismissal of the only generous gesture he had ever made in his life. Although he had had the convent built so that he would always know where she was and so that she would never marry another, it had still been for her that he had done it.

'You made fun of me!' he shouted. 'Both of you laughed at me! Do you know how much that hurts? How much it still hurts. But I'll get you. I know what's in those letters.'

The abbess looked confused. 'I don't know why you're so interested in the letters. They were only about our elopement and, oh . . .' her voice trailed away.

'Yes, "oh"!' he shouted. 'You know why I want them. You know the story!'

'But it's not true,' she said, after a pause. 'None of it is true.'

The Count looked at her triumphantly. 'Oh yes it is! He may have told you he made it up but it was all true.'

'Who? What?' asked Sister Agatha, completely lost. 'What are you talking about?'

She had to shout to be heard, for the fight between the townsmen and the pirates was incredibly loud. Blanco was still staring at her in disbelief and not listening fully to what the Count and the abbess were arguing about. He had really thought that Agatha had liked him but all along she had been spying for the Count, finding out what she could and selling the information on. Well, that was the last time he would ever trust a girl.

Suddenly the Count turned away and grabbed the torch that Griffin still held. He stuck it into the back of the beast.

'No!' cried Blanco, so loudly that even most of the fighters heard and stopped.

It was too late. The flames ignited the firepowder which the Count had already laid within the beast and almost as soon as the torch touched it, it exploded, shooting a ball of fire over the heads of everyone standing there. It was followed by just as big an explosion on the ground as the beast blew up. Everyone stopped fighting to watch as what appeared to be a great, angry dragon flew straight towards the town.

'What was that?'

Micha looked back towards the town. They had stopped flying but were still holding Rameel captive.

'I don't know,' said Rameel. He turned to Azaz. 'What do you think it could be?'

Azaz frowned at Rameel to be quiet.

'Oh, wait a moment,' continued Rameel, putting his finger to his lips as though he had just remembered something. 'Didn't you tell Blanco how to—'

'Rameel,' said Azaz warningly.

'Tell Blanco how to what?' asked Micha. 'What did you do, Azaz?'

'He told Blanco how to finish the Count's experiment,' said Rameel. He then turned to Azaz and smiled sweetly. 'Oh, I'm sorry, was I not supposed to say anything?'

Azaz flew at him but Micha grabbed hold of his robes and pulled him back down to earth.

'You promised you wouldn't interfere,' she said.

'What about you?' retorted Azaz. 'You've been interfering at the convent.'

'At least I didn't cause that!' she said, pointing to where an orange glow of fire could be seen on the horizon.

'But you might have changed things for Blanco and Eva,' he argued back. He knew that he was in the wrong but it only made him even more determined not to admit it.

'How can I have changed things?' she said. 'They're meant to be together.'

'Only because you think so,' shouted Azaz. 'Not everything gets all neatly tied together just because you want it to.'

They were too busy arguing to notice Rameel fly off.

'The convent!' cried the abbess. There was uproar as everyone tried to work out what had just happened. But Blanco heard one voice above the rest.

'Ow! Get off me!'

He turned to find that the Count had Eva in a firm grip.

'I'll kill her if you don't let me go.'

Blanco shrugged.

'Do what you have to,' he said.

'Blanco!' cried the abbess in horror while Eva's eyes filled with tears as she stared at him in disbelief. He looked away and she struggled furiously in the Count's arms.

The Count stared at Blanco over Eva's head trying to frighten him but Blanco had a confident, smug look on his face. The Count looked round and saw that most of the pirates were even now moving in on him in a large circle. There was nowhere for him to go.

'Let her go, Christobal,' said the abbess.

'Let her go,' said Blanco. 'You need her alive.'

The Count's eyes were feverish with a mixture of hate and despair. He tightened his grip on Eva and she cried out.

'Let her go and then raise your arms,' said a voice that only Eva and the Count could hear.

Everyone watching was astounded when the Count abruptly released his hold on Eva and put his arms in the air, but not as astounded as they were when he suddenly rose from the ground and disappeared into the night.

'Witchcraft!' shouted one of the pirates.

'Demons!' shouted another.

The remaining townspeople, already battered by the pirates and horrified by the fires, swore that they would go to church the next day and every day thereafter if only the demons wouldn't steal their souls too.

Magdalena, Eva, and Blanco were left staring at one another.

'You could be more careful,' said the Count from where Rameel had dropped him on the ground.

'It was you or the girl,' said Rameel coldly. 'I think I may have just made the wrong decision.'

The Count stared at where he thought the angel was but he was scared of angering him.

'The order has come,' said Rameel. 'The code has been broken. We must set sail for Venice tonight.'

'But the girl,' said the Count. 'We need to take her with us.'

'Don't worry about the girl,' said Rameel smiling. 'Luca has a plan.'

Chapter 11

Morning brought questions from all quarters. Men had been sent out from the town to find out what had caused the fires that had dropped in from the sky but by the time they got to the launch site, the pirates had long since dispersed and the men who were left were all gabbling about magic and demons. They were quickly taken into custody. The abbess had persuaded Blanco and Eva to hide and then make their way back to the convent. As strangers, they would have been under immediate suspicion and she didn't want to risk their being caught.

There had been little sleeping done, however, for on their return to the convent they had discovered that it was on fire. The Count's aim had been perfect. Thankfully none of the nuns had been injured for they had all been in the chapel at prayers when the fire started.

Blanco, Eva, and Magdalena finally came together in the growing dawn light, their faces black with soot, their eyes red rings of tiredness. As one, they sank down on the wall.

'So, you're Magdalena,' said Blanco, when the silence threatened to stretch on into the next day.

'I was. It's been a long time since I've been called that name though,' said the abbess. She paused and looked at Blanco closely. 'I've been wondering why you would recognize my name. And I've always thought that you looked so familiar. You must be . . . are you . . . ?'

'My great-uncle is Marco Polo,' said Blanco. 'He told me about you.'

She frowned. 'But he's dead,' she said. 'He died on the night we were supposed to elope. His boat capsized.'

This time it was Blanco's turn to frown. 'He's definitely not dead,' he said. 'I've known him all my life.'

'He's famous,' interrupted Eva. 'He wrote this amazing book about his travels. Not Malta though. He never mentioned Malta.'

'No,' said the abbess sadly, all the life gone from her face. 'I see.'

Blanco touched her arm gently. 'I think he thinks you're dead too,' he said. 'He never actually said it but he was very sad when he spoke about you and he really wanted me to get your letters back.'

'Christobal,' said the abbess. 'He was the one who told me that night. I should have known not to believe him.'

'He can be very persuasive,' said Blanco, who had also been tricked by the Count in the past.

'Speaking of the Count,' said Eva staring straight at Blanco, 'one thing I want to know is how did you know *absolutely* that he wasn't going to kill me?' She was still smarting from the memory of Blanco shrugging and turning away when the Count had said he was going to kill her. They had fallen out so many times recently that she really thought that he didn't care any more.

'I knew because I had read his notes,' he said. 'Eva, I don't know if you want to hear this but the Count and the Stranger need you for some experiment they're doing. You're vital to it. He was never going to risk killing you.'

'What?' said Eva, leaping to her feet in fright and looking behind her, as though expecting to be snatched away at any moment. 'Experiment? What do you mean, experiment?'

'I thought maybe you could explain,' said Blanco turning to the abbess. 'It's something to do with the letters that you and my great-uncle sent to each other. Something to do with a legend about lapis lazuli.'

The abbess put an arm round Eva who was still looking frightened. 'You could have put it more gently,' she admonished Blanco.

Blanco looked a little ashamed. Eva did look terrified. He had forgotten just how scared she was of the Stranger, without finding out too that he would stop at nothing to get hold of her. He was about to speak when there was a footfall behind him. Turning, he found himself face to face with a sullen looking Sister Agatha who stood there, eyes downcast, hands demurely clasped in front of her.

'Did you get your money?' he asked bitterly.

'He's not there. He's gone.'

Blanco found it difficult even to look at her. He felt like such a fool.

'Gone where?' demanded Eva when she saw that Blanco wasn't going to say anything.

Sister Agatha shrugged and held out a piece of parchment. 'I found this.'

The abbess stood up and plucked the parchment from Sister Agatha's hand.

'Tell me, Sister Agatha,' she said conversationally.

'Do you really want to get married? Is that why you wanted a dowry so badly?'

Sister Agatha looked at the abbess and decided that she might as well tell the truth. 'No,' she said. 'I don't really want to get married. I just wanted to have some say over what happened to me.'

The abbess nodded at that. Even Eva, although she still hated her, could feel a small spark of sympathy. After all, she had ignored her parents' wishes and done her own thing by running off with Blanco.

'What if I said you could be trained to lead this convent?' said the abbess carefully. 'Under proper instruction, of course.'

Sister Agatha looked at her in complete disbelief. 'You would really let me stay?' she said.

The abbess shrugged. 'I don't want to be in charge any more. The Count promised you money, even if it was for betraying your friends, and this convent is his. Therefore you could try to take charge of it. It's not as easy as it sounds. Look around you.'

Sister Agatha did just that. The convent was in ruins and the nuns were all old and looked lost. She turned back to the abbess.

'I could rebuild it,' she said. 'I could make it work.'

She looked at the three people ranged in front of her. Eva was staring at her in disgust, the abbess in contemplation, and Blanco wouldn't look at her at all. She went over to him.

'I'm sorry, Blanco,' she said, standing in front of him. 'It was a mean thing to do but it was such an opportunity and one I never thought I would have.'

Blanco shrugged and then nodded grudgingly.

Sister Agatha went back to the abbess. 'I will make

this convent work,' she said. 'I'll take instructions from the older nuns and find a way to make it work.'

The abbess nodded. 'Good luck,' she said. 'Perhaps you might like to start now by ordering everyone to go and get some sleep. They've been up all night fighting the fire.'

Sister Agatha nodded and began to walk away. She had only taken a few steps when she turned and looked at Eva. She struggled to get the words out because she disliked Eva as much as Eva disliked her. 'I'm sorry,' was all she said and then she rushed away.

Blanco looked after her for a moment, shook his head, and then turned to the abbess. She had unrolled the parchment that Sister Agatha had found in the Count's laboratory.

Come to Venice, it read. *I have broken the code. LF.*

'Luca Ferron,' said Blanco.

'Who?' said Eva.

'I'm fairly sure it's the Stranger's name,' said Blanco. 'I saw it in the Count's notes.'

Eva turned to the abbess. 'What will you do now?' she asked.

The abbess looked surprised. 'Why, come to Venice with you, of course.'

'There is just one thing,' said Blanco, shuffling his feet and looking awkward. 'Have I mentioned that my great-uncle is married?'

The abbess laughed. 'Don't worry, Blanco. I'm not coming back to stir up trouble between your great-uncle and his wife. I'm coming to fix up the mess that these letters have got us all into.'

'Oh yes,' said Blanco, glad to change the subject. 'You have to tell us what's in them. You can tell us on the way.'

'The way where?' asked Eva.

'The way to Venice, of course.'

'I don't want to go,' she said.

Blanco reached over and took her hand. 'Eva,' he said. 'We have to go. Once Gump is on our side and we're back at home, they'll never be able to attack us or kidnap you. We can find out what they're up to and stop them once and for all. If we keep running, they'll just keep chasing us.'

Eva looked at him, still a little unsure.

'Come on,' he said. 'You know I would never let anything happen to you. What could possibly happen to you in Venice anyway?'

Luca was delighted with how his morning had gone. The wedding plans were going ahead in a most satisfactory way. He had never seen a father so happy to be rid of his child.

Most of all, he was excited about the travel plans he had laid. He and his bride had a long journey in front of them. There was a connection, after all, between the legend and Marco Polo. The heartstone was buried deep within the lapis lazuli mines of Badakhshan, a place where Marco Polo had spent several months when he had first set off on his travels over forty years before.

Luca rubbed his hands together. Yes, it was all going perfectly. Thank goodness for marriage. It made everything legal and he could do what he liked with Eva and there was absolutely nothing that she, or anyone else, could do about it. She was her father's property and once married she became his.

He looked at the letter which lay in front of him, now fully translated. Eva was the key to the heartstone and soon she would belong to him.

All he had to do was wait.

Chapter 12

'Welcome! Welcome! All in favour of free trade are welcome here!'

Thus spoke Antonio, pirate captain, standing at the top of the gangplank and waving at the motley crew to come on board.

'This is Magdalena,' said Eva, as the abbess followed her up the gangplank. She didn't look at all the confident, assured woman that Blanco and Eva knew but instead she looked rather unsure of herself. 'She's the abbess of the convent here.'

It was hard to tell who looked more nervous—Antonio or Magdalena.

'I've never met an abbess before,' said Antonio.

'I've never been on a ship before,' said Magdalena at the same time. They both laughed. 'And I'm not an abbess any more. Please call me Magdalena.'

'And you know Blanco,' said Eva, pushing him forward.

Aunt Hildegard came forward and gave Blanco a big kiss on his cheek which caused him to blush and some of the pirates on deck to snigger loudly. He scowled. Then they cheered. Twenty of them had been there for the big fight at Mdina and they all agreed that they hadn't had such a good punch-up in years. They also hadn't stopped talking about the fire display and the thunder balls and were keen to find out more about them from Blanco. Blanco beamed round at them all.

'Come,' said Aunt Hildegard. 'I'll show you where you will sleep.'

Magdalena was watching the small outline of Malta disappear into the distance.

'Do you wish you hadn't come?' asked Eva, who stood beside her.

Magdalena shook her head. 'No,' she said. 'It was about time I left it behind. Maybe I should have left years ago. It was easier to hide.'

'Is that why you told me you couldn't hide from life in a convent?' asked Eva.

Magdalena nodded.

'Although I suppose you had no other choice,' said Blanco, who stood on her other side, 'since your father had thrown you out. No money, no family. Where would you have gone?'

'Your family!' exclaimed Eva. 'Won't they wonder where you've gone?'

Magdalena shook her head sadly. 'My mother died when I was very young and my father refused to see me after I wouldn't marry Christobal. I heard that he died not long after I went into the convent but I never saw him again.'

'It's too confusing,' said Eva. 'The Count is really Christobal and the Stranger is Luca Ferron. I'll never get used to it.'

Magdalena sighed. 'That was the first time I'd seen Christobal for twenty years. He came back to ask if I'd changed my mind. He turned up without warning and told me all that he had been doing for the last two decades. He said he had been doing it all for me.'

'Did he give you something to drink?' asked Blanco curiously. Magdalena stared at him equally curiously.

'He did,' she said, with surprise. 'Well, at least he tried. How did you know that?'

'Was it the love potion?' interrupted Eva. She turned to Magdalena. 'When I looked at his notes in the laboratory he had all these different recipes for love potions and one of them was heavily marked.'

Magdalena shivered with distaste. 'A love potion?' she said. 'I didn't drink it, thankfully. He told me it was some wine that he had produced that he had named after me. He did get very agitated when I kept refusing.'

Blanco grinned at that, knowing how frustrated the Count would have been.

'I should never have believed him all those years ago when he told me about Marco,' continued Magdalena.

'He must have told Blanco's great-uncle that you had died too,' said Eva persuasively. 'Otherwise he would have come looking for you.'

'Perhaps,' said Magdalena.

'I think the Count is still in love with you,' said Eva.

'And he did build you that convent,' said Blanco, who always felt uncomfortable when the subject of his great-uncle came up.

'He must have loved you very much,' said Aunt Hildegard, who had arrived at the end of the conversation, 'to have done that.'

'I don't think he did that out of love,' said Magdalena. 'I think he wanted to make sure I wouldn't marry anyone else.'

'He should just have snatched you up and run away

with you,' said Antonio, coming up behind them and giving Aunt Hildegard a quick hug. She blushed. Magdalena looked sad. Eva looked at Blanco who quickly looked away.

'I can't believe I'm on another ship with Eva,' he said, trying to change the subject and thereby earning himself a frown from Eva. 'You won't get us thrown off this one, will you?'

Eva scowled ferociously and Magdalena laughed.

'Tell Antonio what you said to the captain of the last ship you were on,' said Aunt Hildegard.

'No,' said Eva.

They all looked at her pleadingly.

'Very well,' she said shortly. 'I called him a squint-eyed pointy-nose and said that if only his leadership was as sharp as his nose then he would have a much more successful ship.'

Antonio roared with laughter. 'No wonder he threw you off.' When he had stopped laughing, he leaned over and said, 'Don't ever threaten my authority on this ship or I won't wait until we're near dry land to throw you overboard.' He was smiling as he said it but everyone there knew that he meant every word.

'Of course she wouldn't,' said Blanco, sorry now that he had ever mentioned it. 'And we're very grateful to you for taking us back to Venice.'

'Let's just say I had some business up that way anyway,' said Antonio. 'And since Hildy asked.'

Hildy? Eva and Blanco couldn't exchange glances for fear that they might laugh. But to hear stern Aunt Hildegard addressed as Hildy was very funny. Then Blanco turned pale and looked over the side. He almost instantly wished that he hadn't for the sight of the waves going up and down mirrored too exactly the sensations he was feeling in his stomach. Eva recognized the signs.

'Tell Aunt Hildegard and Antonio about the flying machine,' she said quickly, hoping that if he got involved in talking about his favourite subject then he wouldn't throw up.

'It was amazing,' said Blanco, a little shakily. 'I felt like a bird. Those miniature flying machines the Count used on Mdina were based on the same design. Remember that compartment in the flying machine, Eva?'

Eva nodded. 'I remember everything about that flying machine. I particularly remember falling to the ground in it and thinking I was going to die.'

'You know,' said Aunt Hildegard sternly, 'when I asked you to look after my niece I didn't think you would be leading her into such danger.'

'Well,' said Blanco, 'I didn't know either and I can only apologize.'

Antonio winked at him. 'Sometimes adventures are hard to resist, aren't they, boy?'

'I'm worried though. From his notebook, that wasn't all the Count is doing,' said Blanco, still trying to keep his mind from the rolling waves. 'There was the beast, although at least that's exploded so he doesn't have it any more. But he was also trying to find a way to make the firepowder help him burrow deep under ground. And he's doing some kind of alchemy and there is something about a special stone of lapis lazuli, hidden deep in the earth. A heartstone, he called it. And it had something to do with yours and Gump's letters, abbess. I mean, Magdalena.'

'I think,' said Eva slowly, 'that it's time Magdalena explained exactly what was in those letters.'

'Later,' said Magdalena, watching her island disappear. 'I'll tell you later.'

Later turned out to be after dinner. Antonio and Aunt Hildegard had insisted on hearing the story as well and they sat patiently with Eva and Blanco waiting for Magdalena to begin.

'To understand why we wrote the letters,' she began, 'you have to understand just how annoying Christobal was.'

'Annoying?' said Blanco. That wasn't the word he would have used to describe the Count—murderous, scheming, and manipulative perhaps, certainly something stronger than annoying.

'He used to follow us all the time. It was difficult enough for Marco and I to spend any time alone.'

'But why was he there in the first place?'

'He was a friend of my father's. They had met on one of my father's numerous voyages and he had invited him to stay. My father wanted him to marry me. He had given up on me by then. I was twenty-five, you see.'

Blanco and Eva nodded seriously. Most girls they knew were married young. They had met because Eva had been sent off to marry a man old enough to be her grandfather.

'But I was out walking the day Christobal arrived and that was when I met Marco. Once I had met him I couldn't look at anyone else.' Her eyes softened as she spoke.

Blanco fidgeted uncomfortably. He still wasn't entirely happy with the fact that Magdalena was coming back to Venice with them. He didn't think that Zia Donata was going to like it at all.

'It's just like Lancelot and Guinevere,' sighed Eva. 'One look was all it took.'

'It was slightly more than that,' said Magdalena with some asperity in her tone. 'I wasn't a complete goose. I liked him because he was intelligent and could tell such interesting stories and he was a lot of fun.' She paused and looked thoughtful for a moment. 'He *was* rather handsome as well,' she added and Eva giggled.

'He is good at telling stories,' agreed Blanco, glossing over the handsome part. 'But what about the letters?'

'Blanco!' exclaimed Eva, shocked at his rudeness.

Magdalena smiled at both of them. She knew that Blanco was feeling uneasy about her talking about his great-uncle in that way.

'I was just coming to them,' she said. 'As I said, it was difficult to get away from Christobal. He was like a puppy trailing at my heels all day. So Marco and I started writing to each other. And then we discovered that Christobal was intercepting the letters and reading them. I couldn't complain to anyone because by then my father had accepted Christobal's offer to marry me. We were engaged even though I didn't want to be.'

'And that's when you decided to write in code?' said Blanco.

'Exactly,' she said. 'We started to correspond with each other about what appeared to be the history and landscape of Malta. But your uncle found a way to write secretly. First of all we used our descriptions of Malta as a code. Then we wrote in an invisible compound. If you dip a piece of parchment in water and then put a dry piece on top and write on it, the words are hidden on the wet parchment underneath when it dries. It can't be read again until it is wet. So we did that. We were planning to elope and couldn't risk Christobal finding out.'

'But why did you need to elope?' asked Eva. 'If your father was so keen for you to marry?'

'He had promised me to Christobal. He didn't like Marco, who had just turned up from nowhere. He called him a liar and a fabricator.'

'Gump is certainly used to being called that,' said Blanco. 'My own father calls him that practically every day.'

'And did the Count work out the code?'

'The one about the landscape, yes, but he knew that there was more going on and it used to make him so frustrated. I think that was when he told my father about me and Marco.

'So, your great-uncle decided to try to distract Christobal as we made our elopement plans. In order to mislead Christobal, in some of the letters he wrote about a legend that he had heard on his travels, about a special stone made of lapis lazuli that is supposed to grant the one who controls it his one true wish. In the "landscape code", he kept alluding to the "key to the hiding place of the heartstone" being hidden in the letters. He even went as far as to describe the location when writing in the invisible ink. I always thought it was false but Christobal seems to think it was true. Clearly he has been searching for a way to find it for twenty years.'

There was no getting away from it. With every passing day they were getting closer to Venice and, for Eva, a horrible reunion with her family.

'And Blanco just doesn't understand,' she said to Magdalena one day as they strolled on the decks. 'I'm worried about what my family are going to do to me. And Blanco knows that the heartstone is what the Count and the Stranger—I mean, Luca—are after and he knows that they need me to help them to get it, yet he never talks about what we're going to do when we get back to Venice. He just keeps saying "Gump will sort it all out". But what if he can't? And why do they need me?'

Magdalena shook her head with frustration. 'I don't know,' she said. 'The legend was all Marco's idea. I know he put in some rhyme about how there was only one person who could retrieve the stone. Maybe Christobal managed to translate that part and you suit it. I'm sorry, Eva. I just don't know. At the time, the "false" legend was the least of my worries.'

'I wish the angels were here,' said Eva.

Magdalena tried not to look surprised by how casually Eva spoke of such great beings. She wasn't entirely sure that she believed in them but she believed that Eva did and so she was willing to agree with her until she was given real proof one way or the other.

'Where are they?' she asked.

Eva shrugged. 'I don't know. They're angry with each other and so they're avoiding each other—and me.'

'I'm sure they'll be back soon,' she said. 'Meanwhile, you could always talk to Blanco.'

'All Blanco cares about are his stupid experiments and what the Count is trying to do,' complained Eva. 'He doesn't really care about me.'

Magdalena looked closely at Eva. She could see that tears were very close to falling.

'If he doesn't watch out,' said Eva, sniffing, 'he'll end up just like the Count.'

Magdalena looked shocked. 'Oh, I'm sure he won't. Christobal is all eaten up with jealousy and bitterness because nothing has turned out the way he wanted it to.'

Magdalena thought as she spoke. Did that mean that she too was eaten up by bitterness because her life had certainly not turned out as she wanted? She had been stuck in a convent while Marco had returned home, married, had a family and become famous. Maybe Christobal hadn't told him she was dead. Maybe he had just left her.

She joined Eva in staring at the horizon, watching for Venice where their fates lay.

Venice

Chapter 13

And then, one day, Venice was within sight.

Blanco was proud of being a Venetian. He knew it was the best city in the world and that the Venetians were the best people. He had looked forward to sailing past the main square of San Marco, along the Mare Adriatico, and round into the Venetian docks. In his head he had envisaged great cheering crowds all along the route, although he hadn't quite worked out what they would be cheering him for.

So it was a great disappointment that, instead of being greeted by a cheering horde, he, Eva, and Magdalena had had to skulk into Venice like lowly criminals. Antonio had docked the ship two leagues south of the city. Even doing that he was taking an enormous risk, for his pirate ship was well known to the Venetian patrols.

'I can't risk it,' he had said, looking genuinely sorry. He had a deeply sentimental streak and had enjoyed hearing the story of Marco, Magdalena, and Christobal and also about the mysterious lapis lazuli heartstone. He had also grown very fond of Blanco, who had shown an inordinate amount of interest in how the ship was steered and how he worked out the wind and had even offered a more accurate way of calculating their best course.

'At least you'll hear what happened,' offered Eva. 'When Magdalena comes back.'

It had been agreed that Magdalena would meet the pirate ship in the same place three days hence and she would return to Malta, although to do what she hadn't quite decided.

Eva was sorry to be saying goodbye to her aunt Hildegard; which wasn't something that she ever thought she would feel. Her aunt had become a much kinder person since marrying Antonio and setting up home on board the pirate ship.

'What will you tell everyone?' she had asked Eva on their last night aboard.

'What do you want me to tell them?'

Aunt Hildegard thought for a moment. 'I think you had better tell them that I was lost at sea in the first pirate attack.' She laughed. 'It's true in a way.'

'Don't walk through there!'

Eva grabbed Magdalena's arm as she was about to walk between two large columns.

'It's bad luck.'

Magdalena walked round the column and into the most amazing square she had ever seen.

Magdalena had never been in Venice before. She had never left Malta and had spent most of their trip up the Adriatic coast exclaiming with wonder at the size of the world and all the wonders it must hold. Although she knew that there were many other countries, and although she had heard all Marco's stories—and all those years ago he had travelled further than anyone—she still couldn't quite believe how much there was to see. Her excitement made Blanco and Eva look at their city anew. Having been away and seen so much else of the world made them realize just how amazing it was.

It was early morning and the market area of the Rialto was bustling with every kind of seller as they passed through. Even Blanco, who didn't want to show too much excitement about being back, couldn't stop himself running to the top of the Rialto Bridge to look down the Grand Canal and see all the gondoliers steering their way in between each other, crossing to the various markets. How had it all managed to stay the same when so much had happened?

'Gump's home is very near here,' said Blanco. 'I'm going to go there first.'

'I don't think I should come with you,' said Magdalena, more nervous than ever at the thought of meeting Marco again after all this time. 'Not until you've informed your great-uncle that I'm here.'

Blanco agreed. 'I thought you could go with Eva to her family's house,' he said. 'She needs a chaperone now that she's back in Venice.'

'You can come with me,' said Eva immediately, 'but I'm not going home.'

'Don't be ridiculous,' said Blanco. 'Of course you are. Where else are you going to go?'

'Anywhere but there,' she said, jutting out her chin. The truth was that she was terrified. She was petrified by being back in Venice knowing that the Count and Luca Ferron were probably here and looking for her. She was also scared about what her family would do to her for not following through with her marriage. She knew they wouldn't believe that Señor Massana had tried to sell her. Also, she had to break the news about

Aunt Hildegard and then she would have to explain that she had travelled unchaperoned across half of Western Christendom with Blanco. All in all, she didn't want to go home. She started with the marriage problem.

'I'm sure Magdalena will help you explain things,' said Blanco, only half listening to her complaints. He couldn't wait to see his great-uncle again. 'I can come round and explain things too. We have to discuss what to do about the Count and Luca Ferron. After I've seen Gump, of course.'

He spoke of Marco as though he would be able to solve all their problems. He had certainly started all of them, thought Eva uncharitably. The Count and Luca Ferron wouldn't be after her if they hadn't believed in that stupid heartstone legend.

Magdalena looked at Blanco in frustration. She could see that Eva desperately needed some reassurance from Blanco that things would be all right and that they would meet up again soon but she could also see that Blanco was blind to all this.

'I'm sure your family will understand things,' she said gently to Eva and gave her a quick hug. Over her shoulder she gave Blanco a quick frown. He looked uncomprehending for a moment and then his face cleared.

'They won't try to marry you off again or anything,' he said, giving Eva's shoulder a rough pat. 'At least, not straightaway. I'll come and see you tomorrow.'

Magdalena raised her eyes to heaven. She supposed that Blanco was just too caught up in all the excitement of coming home to understand that Eva needed a little more than that. Eva looked more worried than ever. She hadn't even considered that they might marry her off again.

'I'm not going,' she said firmly. 'I'll find somewhere to stay and I'll meet you here tomorrow and you can tell me what your great-uncle has decided that we should do.'

'This is stupid,' said Blanco, beginning to lose patience. 'I think—'

But what he thought was never known, for another voice joined the conversation.

'Eva?' it said with some disbelief and a lot of anger. 'What are you doing here?'

They all turned to see a small man standing behind them. He was dressed impeccably and his hair and beard were neatly trimmed. He looked furiously at Eva and then flicked a look at Blanco and Magdalena before looking disdainfully away from them. His cheeks flushed with anger when Eva just stared back in horror.

'Well?' he demanded. 'What do you have to say for yourself?'

Blanco and Magdalena looked at Eva. All the colour had drained from her face.

'Hello, father,' she said.

Blanco felt a little guilty as he walked the short distance from the Rialto Bridge to Gump's house. Eva really had looked shocked, and not very happy, to see her father. At least, he thought, assuaging his guilt slightly, Magdalena had gone with her. To avoid thinking about it further, he tried to work out how long it had been since he had last seen Gump; but since he wasn't quite sure what the date was now, he was having problems.

He knew it had been a long time, maybe even as much as a year. He had missed him terribly and couldn't wait to see him again. So it came as quite a shock when he came under the portico to the house and found that it was all shuttered up. He gazed up at the closed green shutters as though they would open magically and Gump would be waving down at him. He wandered disconsolately on to the bridge which overlooked the house and glanced up and down the canal. Nothing in the murky water gave him a clue. He looked up at the tower of the house, from where he had jumped on more than one occasion, with wings strapped to his body, trying desperately to fly. He had always fallen straight down and had been lucky never to break his neck. Landing in the canal rather than the solid ground had saved him more than once.

He didn't know what to do next. Like Eva, he didn't really want to go straight home and he began to feel a little more sympathy for her predicament. He had been so sure that Gump would be here—he was always here—that he hadn't thought what he would do if he wasn't.

He was just about to go and see whether any of Gump's daughters knew where he was when he heard footsteps coming through the square which led to the portico. A moment later, Gump's familiar face appeared, with Zia Donata following a little way behind.

'What do you want?' growled Gump when he saw a boy sitting on the bridge by his house. 'I'm not interested in buying anything.'

Blanco laughed and stood up. He now towered over his great-uncle, so he must have grown on his trip.

'Gump, it's me!'

'Me who?' said Gump grumpily. 'Wait a moment.'

He fished in his pockets and eventually extracted two small roundels of glass, connected only with a piece of metal, which he balanced on his nose. Recognition dawned in his eyes as Zia Donata appeared at his shoulder and exclaimed:

'Blanco! Good gracious! We never expected to see you again!'

Seated round a heavily laden table—Zia Donata knew her great-nephew well—Blanco finally got a chance to tell all that had happened to him since he had last seen them. It was difficult for he had to give a heavily edited version. Zia Donata showed no signs of leaving the room and so Blanco had to leave out all mention of letters, codes, and, especially, Magdalena.

'I like the sound of Eva,' she said when Blanco mentioned how they had met on the ship. 'I hope you took her to her fiancé like you promised.'

Again Blanco had been highly selective in his account and hadn't mentioned Eva's angels, which he didn't think Zia Donata would like quite so much.

He continued with his tale of the journey. He had just got to the castle and was wondering how much to tell them. It was difficult. If he didn't mention the letters then it all sounded like a fuss over nothing and he couldn't see Zia Donata believing that two grown men would want to kill him because he had found out that they were developing a secret to do with firepowder. Had he known it was going to be this complicated he would have waited and caught Gump alone!

'I am so sorry, Blanco,' said Zia Donata, cutting right

across his description of the amazing feast that they had eaten on their first night at the Count's castle, 'but I'm afraid that I am going to have to go out. I promised Fantina that I would help her with the meal she is preparing for her husband's family.' Fantina was Gump and Zia Donata's youngest daughter and she continually needed her mother's advice.

'I can tell you the rest later,' said Blanco, trying to hide his relief as she bustled about the room.

She waved airily. She had already heard enough tales of travels from her husband and she couldn't imagine that Blanco had much new to add. Gump and Blanco sat in silence at the table as she wrapped her shawl about her.

'Oh, Zia Donata!' called Blanco, just as she was going out of the door. She popped her head back in. 'You won't tell my father I'm back, will you?'

She stared at him quizzically and then sighed. 'You are going to see him?'

'Oh, of course,' said Blanco. 'It's just I'd rather wait for now.'

'Very well,' she said. 'But make sure you go soon. I think you'll find there have been some changes since you've been gone.'

And with that she herself was gone, shutting the door loudly behind her. Blanco and Gump looked at each other.

'So,' said the old man, leaning across the table, his eyes twinkling with fun. 'Are you going to tell me what really happened now?'

'I got to fly, you were right about the Count, he tried to kill me, and Eva, and I've met M—'

'Slow down, boy,' said Gump smiling. 'No need to

tell me all in one sentence. What's all this about the Count trying to kill you? Or, no, tell me about the flying machine first.'

Blanco had been about to tell Gump about meeting Magdalena but his mention of the flying machine put all such thoughts out of his head. The telling of how he helped build it led on inevitably to how the Count had tried to kill him and Eva and how they had eluded him by flying out of the window.

'I knew I should never have let you go,' said Gump sighing. 'Some people never change and I should have known the Count was one of them.'

'You mean Christobal Vellatin?' said Blanco slowly, now that his initial excitement had worn off and he remembered the trouble they were in.

Gump's mouth fell open in astonishment. 'Now, how in the name of all the saints did you find that out? I can't believe that *he* told you.'

Blanco paused in his headlong rush to tell everything all at once. There was so much he still had to say but he knew that there was one thing that he could not put off any longer.

'He didn't. There's something else I have to tell you, Gump.'

'What's that, boy?'

'I met Magdalena.'

Chapter 14

Eva's family weren't very interested in her explanations and they certainly would not have been pleased if the word 'angels' ever crossed her lips. The 'angels' had been the reason, after all, why they had tried to marry her off. She and Magdalena had been taken into the formal family room by Eva's father and there she had faced all her relatives. Round the walls were dark paintings of martyred saints suffering all kinds of agonies and torments. Even the light coming through the window seemed dimmed by the gloom within. Eva had always hated this room and it seemed to have become darker and grimmer since she had been away.

Her father, mother, sister, her sister's husband, and an assortment of aunts and uncles all stared at her with a variety of expressions, ranging from disappointment and anger to disgust. Not one of them looked at her pleasantly or even remotely sympathetically. Certainly none of them looked pleased to see her. She tried to catch the eye of her sister, but Giuliana steadfastly refused to respond with any friendliness.

'Do you have any idea,' asked her father through gritted teeth, 'of the shame and humiliation that your actions have put us through?'

Eva stared at him mutely. She was sitting on a hard,

high-backed chair facing them all and she fidgeted as her discomfort increased.

'Well?' asked her mother, when the silence grew too long. 'Do you have nothing to say?'

Eva opened her mouth. As one her whole family sat forward, listening intently for what she might have to say. She shut it again and they all sat back. Magdalena hid a small smile.

Eva's father sighed loudly and then unrolled a piece of parchment which he had been clenching in his hand.

Greetings to Signor di Montini and his family from Señor Massana and his family, once esteemed partner in business, bearing news of your daughter, Eva di Montini.

Here Signor di Montini paused and looked at Eva. She stared at him, dreading what was coming, for it could be nothing good, of that she was sure. She tried to smile jauntily, but it was a trifle tremulous. He glared at her through narrowed eyes and then looked down again.

It is with pleasure that I can inform you that your daughter arrived safely in Barcelona, despite having been delayed by a pirate attack and then having to walk over the Pyrenees in order to reach here. It is my understanding that she also had a stay of some time at the residence of a certain Count Maleficio, a delightful man and welcoming host. Unfortunately your daughter, while staying there in the company of a young gentleman called Blanco Polo, who had been accompanying her on her travels, caused the total destruction of his castle.

'You should be ashamed,' hissed one of the aunts.

'Travelling without a chaperone, in the company of a young man,' snapped another.

'Destroying property!' shouted an uncle. 'That is truly despicable!'

'Who was this boy?' asked her mother.

'And where's my aunt Hildegard?' asked her sister, Giuliana.

'Lost at sea,' replied Eva promptly. It was the one thing she felt she could say safely.

'There is more!' announced her father and an expectant silence fell over the room.

Despite her unconventional arrival, she settled in quite easily and the wedding preparations went ahead as planned. My grandmother and my cousin Maria had spent months preparing the wedding garments and did their best to make Eva feel part of the family.

Here Eva snorted loudly, although she did her best to turn it into a cough. That did not quite tally with her memories of scheming cousin Maria but she knew her family would not be interested in what she thought.

On the day of our proposed nuptials, my grandmother dressed Eva in her wedding gown and left her in the private chapel to say her prayers. When she returned she found that Eva had disappeared—it is believed with the young man, Blanco Polo. We have not seen or heard from her since.

'Disgusting behaviour,' said her sister's husband. 'I can tell that I married the right sister.'

Since Eva had always thought that her sister's husband was an odious, sly, manipulative fool, she also felt that he had made the correct choice. She glowered at him but then turned back to her father as he finished the letter.

Needless to say, our family no longer has any desire to continue trading with you and will be informing your other business contacts and advising them likewise. If you cannot control your own daughter then it is unlikely that you can control your business.

Here Signor di Montini stopped, crumpled the parchment and threw it to the floor. Apart from that the room remained in total silence.

'Explain yourself, daughter!' he suddenly roared.

'If I could just . . .' started Magdalena.

'Madam,' thundered Signor di Montini, 'I pray for silence from you on this matter. Indeed on any matter!'

Magdalena was just about to tell him exactly what she thought of him speaking to her in that manner when she was interrupted by a cry from Eva.

'They're here!' she wailed in a frightening manner. 'They're here! The angels!'

She pointed dramatically to a spot in the far corner, just behind where most of the family were sitting. Her sister and one of the aunts leapt to their feet and scuttled to the other side of the room. The rest stayed where they were but looked a little nervous.

Magdalena watched in astonishment as Eva collapsed on the floor and writhed about.

'This is ridiculous,' said Signor di Montini eventually. 'I can see we will get no answers from you today. We will leave you to regain your senses.' He motioned for the rest of the family to go out of the room ahead of him and with a cold look at Eva he left, locking the door firmly behind him.

Blanco was not very happy. When Gump had heard that Blanco had not only met Magdalena but that she had returned to Venice with him, he was furious. So furious, in fact, that he had thrown Blanco out of the house. So now a bewildered Blanco stood, back on the Rialto Bridge, gnawing on his lip and wondering what to do next. He watched the gondolas and barges as they plied their trade up and down the Grand Canal. Crammed full of cloths, spices, oranges, saffron, salt and other spices they made bright and exotic splashes against the limpid green of the canal's water. Watching the wares go by, his mind turned again to the lapis lazuli stone that Luca Ferron and Count Maleficio wanted so desperately. Just how far would they go to get it?

The Count climbed the steps with a mixture of feelings. He had good news to report in the form of the firepowder but he was furious that Blanco was still alive. And even though Rameel had told him that Luca had a foolproof idea for capturing Eva, he still wished that he had been the one to have brought her back. He sometimes felt that he was working *for* Luca rather than *with* him. When they had first met, the Count had had the upper hand since he knew about Marco's letters and had developed the ideas for using the firepowder and flying machines to help them retrieve the stone. But somewhere along the way Luca seemed to have taken charge and the Count felt that it was time that he redressed the balance. He was the one who had taken all the risks—stealing the letters, building the flying machine, and trying out the firepowder—while Luca sat in luxury in his apartment in Venice.

He pushed open the heavy, ornately carved wooden door and walked in. Luca stood over at the far window, looking out on to the canal. He turned as he heard the Count come in.

'Maleficio,' he said, his face wreathed in its usual big

smile, making him look like a jolly old man, 'or should I say Christobal.'

The Count scowled. 'I prefer Maleficio,' he said. 'That's why I chose it.'

'Of course, of course,' said Luca soothingly, although the Count was sure that he could still detect a mocking tone. He began to get angry.

The Count looked round the opulent surroundings. The room was stuffed full of furniture and wall hangings and there were heavy silk curtains on the window.

'Please,' said Luca, motioning the Count to the nearest chair, 'have a seat. You've had a long journey. I'll have some food brought up.' He rang an unseen bell.

The Count felt slightly mollified and settled himself on a red damask chair. 'You wrote that you broke the code?'

Luca nodded, beaming. 'You were right. It was in the second set of letters. The first contained no code. The second held two. The first code, the one you cracked, was about about elopement plans.' Here he raised an eyebrow. 'About which I presume you knew since the marriage never happened?'

The Count scowled and Luca moved on, delighted that he now had something else with which to needle the Count. He was so ridiculously easy to rile that it was no challenge, but it was such fun.

'And the second?'

'It is as we thought. It tells us the location of the stone.'

The Count leaned forward excitedly. 'Where is it?'

'A long way away,' said Luca, his smile fading a little at the thought. He was a man who enjoyed his luxuries and, even though he could take as many of them as he liked when he travelled, it wasn't quite the same. 'We have to retrace the steps of Marco Polo.'

The Count frowned at the sound of his rival's name. 'Do we still need the girl?'

'Of course,' said Luca. 'She is, as we say in alchemy, the divine spark.'

'Rameel said you have a plan?'

A servant entered with a tray bearing food and drink. He placed it on a small table by the Count.

Luca leaned forward and tapped the Count on the knee. 'How,' he said, 'would you like to come to a wedding?'

'A wedding?' asked the Count, confused by the change in topic.

Luca smiled. '*My* wedding. Who do we know who failed to attend her first marriage?'

A slow smile spread across the Count's face, creasing his scar, hurting him. He rubbed it unconsciously. 'Wonderful,' he said. 'Perfect.' For, on top of everything else, he knew just how much it would hurt Blanco.

Luca had picked up one of the tankards and taken a sip. He spat out the contents and threw the full tankard at the retreating servant. 'When I say hot, I mean hot!' he shouted.

The Count looked amazed at Luca's tankard. He had never seen Luca lose his equilibrium before and he stored the knowledge up for future use.

'Now I must go,' said Luca. 'I have a dinner appointment.'

Once he had gone the Count crossed the room and rifled through Luca's desk. He wanted to read the translated letters himself. He didn't trust Luca to tell him the truth. He had already left Griffin on Luca's ornate ship to see what he could find out from the crew. No, he really didn't trust him at all.

Blanco mounted the steps mournfully. He had whiled away as much time as he could wandering through the little back streets, seeing if he could remember them as well as he used to. He had got lost only twice and even then he knew he had done it deliberately to delay the inevitable. But finally there was no other alternative. He was going to have to go home. He had hoped that when he made his first appearance he would have Gump by his side. He still couldn't fully understand why Gump had thrown him out. He had obviously got a shock when Blanco said that Magdalena was in Venice but it was rather unfair of him to blame Blanco for that. It wasn't as though he hadn't done his best to warn Magdalena that it was a bad idea.

So here he was, standing outside the door to his father's house, alone. At least he would get to see his mother. He had missed her while on his travels. He also cheered himself up by hoping that his sister Angelica had been married off while he was away and so wouldn't be there. He gave himself a shake. He had faced pirates, murderers, and firepowder on his journey so far. It was ridiculous to think that his father would still be able to scare him. He squared his shoulders and pushed open the door.

The last person that Blanco had expected to see sitting at his father's dinner table was Luca Ferron. One by one every hair on his head stood on end. He hadn't set eyes on Luca since Barcelona and he had forgotten how he looked. He was, as he had always been at the castle, smiling. But Blanco now noticed that the smile never quite reached the centre of his eyes. He had a way of making them twinkle so that it seemed he was smiling happily but deep in their centres lay a cold, dark well of nothingness. He seemed very pleased and not at all surprised to see Blanco—almost as though he had been expecting him.

That was shock enough but when Blanco managed to tear his eyes away from Luca Ferron he found that it was only the first shock of many. His mother, who sat to the right of Luca, was half the size she had been when he had last seen her and was smiling happily. His father, on the other hand, who sat to Luca's left, looked miserable and unhappy and old, much older than Blanco remembered. He looked, and then looked again, to be completely sure of the identity of the fourth person at the table. At first he had thought it a young boy, maybe an apprentice that his father had taken on, but he was dressed far too smartly for that and, besides, his father never let the apprentices sit at the dinner table with the family. He had always said it bred too much familiarity. It was only when he looked a third time that he realized it was his sister, Angelica. Her hair was shorn and she was attired in boys' clothing. What, in the name of St Mark, was going on? How had Angelica got their father to agree to this?

He stood there, frozen between trying to take it all in and fear at the sight of Luca. Nobody had noticed him yet and the talk continued round the table. It was of trade routes and money and all the things that Blanco had been so glad to leave behind when he had gone away all those months ago. Maybe he could just sneak away again. Then he realized that while none of his family had seen him, Luca Ferron certainly had and even as he continued a conversation with Blanco's mother, his eyes were twinkling at Blanco in a way that he remembered all too clearly and had never liked.

'Well, come in, boy,' Luca said suddenly, turning his full gaze on Blanco. 'Don't stand there loitering.'

His words caused everyone else to stop talking and they all, with one accord, turned to face the doorway. There was sudden, constant babble. Blanco could not make out a word and, in fact, found it difficult to work out whether he was being welcomed back or being shouted at. He rather suspected that it was the latter. His father eventually thumped on the table and silence descended.

'Who is it?' he asked in a querulous voice. 'What's going on?'

'It's me, father!' said Blanco. Surely he hadn't been away so long that his own father no longer recognized him. 'Blanco.'

'Blanco?' repeated his father, appearing confused and not looking straight at him.

'Your son,' said Blanco, slightly impatiently. What was the matter?

His mother got up and came round to give him a hug.

'It's lovely to see you back, Blanco,' she said. 'Did you have a nice trip?'

Blanco wasn't quite sure how to react to that. He couldn't tell them what had happened, since Luca Ferron was sitting smiling at him. And his mother was speaking to him as though he had just been for a long walk, not been gone for months.

'Yes,' he replied hesitantly. 'You look wonderful, mother.'

'Thank you,' she said, hugging him again.

'Hello, Blanco,' said Angelica coolly when his mother had released him.

'Hello, Angelica,' he replied warily. She had that look in her eyes that he remembered from childhood. It usually meant that she would hit him if he didn't do what she said. 'How do you like my dress? Don't you think the green suits me?'

Blanco stared at her in confusion. She was dressed in a bright blue doublet. She frowned at him and then at her father. Blanco realized that she was telling him that their father did not know that she was dressed in boys' clothing. He had gone blind.

'It's lovely,' he said hesitantly. He cast her a scandalized look as he said it. He had never seen a girl dressed in boy's clothing before and it seemed shocking. She smiled at him coldly and turned back to her dinner.

'Is it really Blanco?' asked his father, who had remained seated at his place at the table. 'Bring him round here.'

His mother took him by the arm and round to his father. Signor Taddei put out a hand and touched Blanco's face. Blanco flinched, expecting to be struck. He had left home without permission and had made no effort to contact them since. But, instead of being struck, he stood in shock and surprise as his father caressed his face, his eyes filling with tears.

Blanco then turned to Luca Ferron who smiled benignly at him.

'What are you doing here?' he demanded, trying to feel brave.

'Blanco!' said Angelica in horror. 'Señor Ferron is one of our—of the business's—most important trading partners.'

'But . . .'

'It's lovely to see you again, Blanco,' said Luca. 'I was just about to tell your family that you and I had met during your travels. They were concerned, having heard nothing from you and I was happy to know that I would be able to tell them that you were still alive. And now here you are in person!'

Blanco stared at him. If he was alive it was only because he had managed to escape from the man sitting across from him. The silence stretched out.

'Is there something wrong?' asked his father nervously. 'What's going on?'

This, thought Blanco, was hardly the time to mention that their esteemed dinner guest had tried to kill him a few months before. He sat down beside his father and contented himself with glaring across the table. Luca responded with the kind of smile that sent shivers down Blanco's spine and then he turned to Angelica.

'As I was saying just before your brother returned—and isn't his timing fortuitous, for I think he will like this—I have some good news.' Spearing himself a piece of meat from the centre of the table and smiling round at them all, he announced: 'I am to be married.'

Chapter 15

'So now what?' asked Magdalena.

'Well,' said Eva, settling herself more comfortably on the window seat so that she could look out properly. 'Normally they leave me alone for a day when I have one of my attacks.'

'Speaking of which,' said Magdalena, 'what *were* you doing?'

Eva laughed. 'I told you that they sent me away to get married to Señor Massana because of my angels. They, of course, don't think that they are angels—they think they are demons trying to tempt me, and so sometimes I play along just for the fun of it.'

Magdalena shook her head. 'You do make things difficult for yourself, Eva,' she said. 'So the angels aren't really here?'

'Oh, they're here,' said Eva. 'It's just that you can't see them.'

'Where?'

'Azaz is in the corner.'

Unseen by Magdalena Azaz raised a lazy hand and waved.

'And Micha is on the settle.'

Micha smiled. She liked Magdalena. She liked that she had kept true to her dream of Marco. She glanced over at

Azaz but looked away just as quickly as he looked at her. They were still not speaking.

Eva frowned when she saw how the angels were behaving with each other. She still didn't know what had happened between them but if they were just going to ignore each other she was sure that she didn't want to get caught in the middle.

'Anyway, it means they left us alone,' replied Eva defiantly. 'Otherwise they would have lectured me for hours and they might even have sent me away again straight away. Now at least we have time.'

'Time for what?'

'To escape, of course.'

A new day brought a fresh onslaught of di Montini relatives. They came in pairs and groups, all of them intent on talking to Eva, but she thwarted them by pretending to be in a deep sleep. Magdalena they ignored completely, even if she tried to speak to them. Eventually, Eva's father came and stood looking down at her.

'Eva.' She slept on. 'Very well,' he said, turning to Magdalena who was sitting by Eva's bed. 'Signora,' he said coldly. 'I must ask you to come with me.'

Magdalena looked at him with surprise. She was so used to being ignored by them all that it had taken her a moment to realize that he was, in fact, talking to her. She laid aside the sewing that she had been doing to pass the time and raised an eyebrow. 'Where, may I ask, do you intend to take me?'

'My sister has offered to accommodate you at her house,' he said. 'You are no longer welcome here.'

'Father!' said Eva, sitting bolt upright and sounding scandalized.

'I am not prepared to leave Eva,' said Magdalena calmly.

'Really,' said Signor di Montini, not sounding in the least bit surprised. He clicked his fingers and two servants entered. 'These men will escort you to my sister's house. I trust you will not make a scene.'

Magdalena had never in all her life been treated in this way. Having gone from being the only daughter of a noble family to being the abbess of a convent, she had always been extended every courtesy and respect. But she was aware that she was in a strange country with different customs and, more to the point, with no one to come to her assistance. At least no one in this house. She glanced at Eva, who was looking horrified.

'In that case, I'm going with her,' said Eva, scrambling out of bed.

Her father pushed her back. 'You're staying here.' He nodded towards Magdalena. 'Escort her out,' he said to the servants.

Magdalena took both of Eva's hands in her own. Eva's were frighteningly cold.

'I will come back,' said Magdalena. She lowered her voice. 'With friends.'

Eva nodded.

'Come, signora,' said Signor Taddei impatiently. 'I wish to speak with my daughter alone.'

'I will leave,' she said, turning to him, 'but I will not be staying with your sister. I shall make my own arrangements.' She swept from the room.

'The angels are here,' said Eva defiantly as Magdalena left the room.

Her father smiled a cold, strange little smile.

'You can bring them down with you,' he said. 'Your new fiancé doesn't seem to mind them. In fact, he can't wait to meet them.'

Azaz and Micha came from their separate sides of the room and stood, one on each side, behind her.

'Don't worry,' said Micha.

'I'll look after you,' said Azaz.

Micha snorted with disbelief and Azaz shot her a furious look.

'This is not about you,' he said furiously and Micha had the grace to look ashamed.

Eva frowned at the angels and then at her father but reluctantly got to her feet and followed him downstairs. She had no doubt that her father would have no hesitation in ordering the servants to carry her otherwise. She followed him slowly. She had a terrible feeling about who she would see when the door to the great hall was opened.

'Hello, Eva,' said a familiar face as her father pushed her into the room in front of him.

The Stranger was standing in front of the window and the light streaming in from outside cast him into shadow but his voice was exactly as she remembered. He stepped forward and she saw that he was smiling as broadly as he had been on the night they had first met at the Count's castle. Eva opened her mouth to speak, but terror struck her dumb and then she fainted dead away.

'Why didn't you tell me any of this?' Blanco asked furiously.

'When was I supposed to tell you? You kept babbling on about all that you had done. You didn't think that things might have moved on here without you?'

After a very disturbed and disturbing night, Blanco had made his way straight back to Gump's house. He had had to spend an entire meal pretending that Angelica was not dressed as a boy. Then he had had to eat with only one hand, for his father had refused to let go of his other one. And, finally, he had had to show no fear of Luca Ferron and try to ignore the fact that, the last time that they had met, Luca had tried to kill him.

Gump looked quite happy to see Blanco the next morning—or at least he did until Blanco started shouting at him. It wasn't long before Gump started shouting back, blaming Blanco for the return of Magdalena and for being away so long and for never sending letters to let him know that everything was well. It took quite a while for either of them to realize that neither could hear the other, they were both shouting so loudly. Shamefaced, they fell silent. Gump motioned for Blanco to speak.

'What is going on at home?' Blanco asked.

Gump sighed and pushed a goblet of watered wine over to Blanco.

'It all began when you went away,' he said. 'Not that I'm blaming you,' he added hastily as he saw Blanco open his mouth in protest. 'It might have happened anyway. The saints know that you upset him often enough in the past.'

Blanco looked confused.

'It was when he found out that you had disappeared. Your father was furious and started ranting and shouting and calling you all kinds of names.' Gump paused. 'I had no idea just how extensive his vocabulary was.'

'Gump,' said Blanco warningly.

'Well, he turned red and then just fell down and started frothing at the mouth. It was as though he had been attacked by a demon.'

'As soon as he found out I was gone?'

'Maybe a week later,' said Gump. 'He didn't wake up for a week after that and when he did, he couldn't see.'

'What, nothing? One week he could see and the next nothing?'

Gump nodded solemnly. 'I know you two never agreed with each other,' he said, 'and I had no great fondness for him myself, but even his stoutest enemy would not have wished this on him.'

Blanco paused for a moment before replying. His father had some fierce enemies and he didn't entirely share Gump's conviction that none of them would have wished this on him but he did know that *he* would never have wished it. They had their differences, it was true, but to be unable to see anything?

'But his business?' he gasped as that thought emerged in his mind. 'What about his business? How can he see if someone is trying to cheat him?'

'Ah,' said Gump, meditatively stroking his beard, 'this is where we come to your sister.'

Blanco listened in astonishment as Gump explained how Angelica had decided to take over the business. Knowing that their father was strictly against females in business she was pretending to be their cousin Giacomo. Signor Taddei's brother had a similar business on the Tyre leg of the trade route and had three sons. Angelica was pretending to be the middle one, sent by his father to help out while Blanco's father was ill. Blanco shook his head in amazement at her audacity.

'Has no one told father what she's doing?'

'No,' said Gump. 'No one has guessed yet. She's very good at what she does actually. Your mother knows, of course.'

Angelica would be happy now. She had always wanted to run the business and had been furious that their father had never let her. Blanco should have been pleased since he had never wanted anything to do with the business but he couldn't help feeling that something had been stolen from him.

'As for your mother, she's been like a new woman since your father fell ill,' said Gump affectionately. 'I think it's because she has something to do now, looking after him. And she fully supports Angelica. All in all, your leaving was the best thing that ever happened to them.'

Blanco sat in stunned silence at this and found that he could not refute Gump's words. He felt disgruntled. Was he that unimportant to them all? He rested his chin on his hand and thought.

'Of course,' continued Gump conversationally, 'I missed you, boy.'

This remark sank through Blanco's gloomy thoughts like a ray of sunshine. He grinned at his uncle and, as he looked at him, he thought of all that he had done since he had left home and all that was still to come. Eva and Magdalena, the Count and Luca Ferron, the angels and the lapis lazuli. He felt a small pang of guilt as he thought about Eva. He had barely spared her a thought since yesterday. He wondered how she was getting on with her family and if she had found as many changes as he had.

'What are we going to do about the letters?' Blanco asked. 'The Count and Luca Ferron really believe them, Gump. They really believe there is a special lapis lazuli. And they think that Eva is the only one who can get it. And what about Magdalena? And why is Luca Ferron at my house anyway? I have to warn Eva—and Magdalena.'

'We'd better go and speak to her,' said Gump heavily. 'Where is she staying?'

'She's with Eva,' said Blanco.

At that moment he felt the familiar burning sensation and a voice spoke in his ear.

'You must come!'

'Azaz! What is it?'

'Azaz?' said Gump. 'What are you saying? Who are you talking to?'

'It's Eva,' said Azaz. 'She's in danger.'

'Where?'

All Gump could see was his nephew talking to a place on the wall where the shield that he had received from the Great Khan hung. He looked closer. If he squinted, he thought there might be a red glow around the shield but nothing else.

'Blanco?' he asked questioningly.

'It's Eva! We have to go. Right now.'

'Signorina di Montini is not here,' said the man who answered the door.

Blanco had been shocked when he discovered where Eva lived. It was one of the most opulent palazzi in Venice and her father turned out to be one of the richest merchants in the city. Having only ever seen her in a somewhat dishevelled state, and content whether sleeping out under the stars or in a shed, Blanco had always assumed that she came from a smaller merchant's family like his own. He quickly learned that it was not so.

The man made to close the door. Gump put his foot in the way to prevent it from shutting.

'Perhaps,' he said sweetly, 'you could tell us where Signorina di Montini is if she is not here.'

'I am not at liberty to disclose the whereabouts of any of the di Montini family,' he said, with a look that said precisely what he thought of the two of them daring to ask for any member of the said family. So saying, he kicked Gump's foot out of the way and slammed the door shut.

'Nice family you're mixed up with,' said Gump meditatively.

'Eva's not like that,' said Blanco, craning his neck upwards, trying to see in one of the windows. 'Not like that at all. I didn't even know she was from such a rich family and, trust me, when you meet her, you won't believe it either.' He could see nothing. The shutters were drawn across most of the windows. Those where they weren't had balconies in front of them, which blocked his view.

'Do you think she's in there?' asked Gump.

'Definitely,' replied Blanco. 'Where else would she be? We only came back yesterday.'

Magdalena and Zia Donata were enjoying some wine and olives and looked up with surprise as Gump, followed closely by Blanco, stumbled into the kitchen.

'Ah, here you are, my dear,' said Zia Donata. 'This

lady was looking for you or Blanco. She's come all the way from Malta, she says.'

Gump appeared to have been struck dumb, though whether it was from the shock of seeing Magdalena after all these years or because Magdalena was talking to Zia Donata, Blanco was not quite sure. He stood there with his mouth hanging open and no sound coming out.

Zia Donata got up from her seat.

'Blanco,' she said. 'I wonder if you would help me. I need something down from the top of the chest upstairs and I can't reach.'

She motioned for him to follow her and disappeared up the stairs. Blanco grimaced but did as his great-aunt bid. As he passed Gump, the old man put out a hand as though to stop him but withdrew it just before they made contact. Instead he waved him in the direction of Zia Donata and the stairs. Blanco looked from Gump to Magdalena and then shrugged and followed his aunt upstairs.

'Hello, Marco.'

Gump had been looking fixedly at the floor since Blanco had left the room but at Magdalena's words he raised his eyes and smiled at her. She looked different from what he had expected. Not only because she had aged but also because she looked tired and more than a little sad, as though life had disappointed her. She in her turn thought that he looked happy and healthy and while she was pleased for him she couldn't help feeling that life had treated her unfairly in comparison.

'Magdalena,' he said. 'I never thought I would ever see you again.'

She smiled a little ruefully at that. 'Neither did I,' she said. 'But then, I was told that you had died.'

'And I you,' he countered.

'Christobal,' they both said.

They stared at each other, unsure of what to say next. Could they discuss what had passed between them twenty years before when Zia Donata was upstairs? And how did that affect how they were now? Were they not both different people from who they had been then?

'Blanco is a wonderful boy,' said Magdalena when the silence threatened to grow too long.

'He is,' agreed Marco, thankful to seize on such an easy topic of conversation. 'But we seem to have got him and his friend into rather a lot of trouble.'

'The letters,' said Magdalena.

'The letters,' agreed Gump.

'What are we going to do, Marco?'

'I don't know.'

There was a sudden clattering down the stairs and they both turned to see Blanco arrive at the bottom, Zia Donata calling after him from the top.

'I've just realized,' he said, gasping from his sudden descent, 'how they're going to get Eva.'

Gump and Magdalena stared at him blankly.

'He's going to marry her,' said Blanco. 'We have to stop him.'

'Azaz.'

Azaz looked up. Micha was hovering above him. He was sitting by the side of the Rialto Bridge watching everyone pass and shout and laugh and sing and wondered, not for the first time, what it would be like to be human.

'What?' he said crossly. Micha had been lecturing him almost non-stop since they had returned from Malta and he was tired of listening to her. He knew that he had done wrong but he didn't see how her shouting at him would make it any better.

Micha continued to hover.

'Did you tell Blanco?' she asked. She was almost ready to forgive Azaz for what he had done. He seemed to have learnt his lesson.

Azaz, thinking he was going to get another lecture, nodded and then looked at her with cold eyes. 'Why don't you go away?' he said. 'Leave Eva to me. I work better alone.'

Micha's eyes filled with tears and she flew away, not looking where she was going, and therefore straight into Rameel's trap.

Chapter 16

Eva was frantic. Where was Blanco? She had sent Azaz off to tell him a couple of days ago. She looked down at herself in yet another wedding dress. The last time she had worn one she had wanted to get married— although she was now glad that she hadn't. But this time she knew she didn't want to wear it.

She heard the door being unbolted and waited to see who would come in. She had been largely left alone since two days before when she had been introduced to her fiancé. As she discovered, the wedding had been planned for weeks, the banns had been called, and her family were in full agreement. And there was absolutely nothing she could do. If she didn't get out of this house then she would have to marry Luca Ferron tomorrow.

Her sister, Giuliana, came in carrying a velvet case full of jewellery. 'Now let's see what will match the dress,' she said, putting it down on the bed and starting to take pieces from it, holding them up against Eva's dress. Eva grabbed her hand and forced her sister to look her in the eye.

'Giuliana, you have to help me. I don't want to get married.'

Giuliana looked at Eva with unfriendly eyes. 'I didn't

want to get married either,' she said, 'and nobody helped me.'

Eva looked at her with surprise. Giuliana had always been the perfect daughter and she had always seemed to be happy with the plans that their parents had made for her.

'I thought you were happy,' said Eva.

Giuliana shrugged. 'I've made myself content,' she said. 'It's not the same thing.'

'But, Giuliana,' said Eva eagerly, 'that means you wouldn't want me not to be happy. Just get me out of this room and I'll always be grateful.'

Giuliana gave her a chilly smile and stepped back. 'No,' she said in a considered manner. 'I think it would be much less bother all round if you got married. We all have to go through it and I don't see why things should be any different for you. I know you think you're special, Eva, but it's about time you realized that you are just the same as the rest of us.'

'But he doesn't really want to marry me,' said Eva. 'He wants to kill me.'

Giuliana gave a weary sigh. 'Oh, not more stories. I thought you'd grown out of them.'

'Please, Giuliana,' pleaded Eva. 'At least take a message for me.'

Giuliana picked up the jewellery tray and walked over to the door.

'This is what the rest of your life is going to be like, Eva,' she said. 'Having to do things that you don't want to. You'd better become accustomed to it.'

She opened the door and then closed it behind her. Eva heard the heavy bolt thud shut.

'I hope you haven't come back to spoil things.'

The voice came from behind Blanco and he didn't recognize it at first. He was walking back to his own house, having left Magdalena with Gump and Zia Donata. They still had to come up with an idea for saving Eva and Blanco was deep in his thoughts when he heard the voice. It had grown dark as he walked the short distance between Gump's house and his own and the shadows were deep. His first instinct was to reach for the knife which hung on his belt, fearing that it was either the Count or Luca Ferron. But the voice was too high for either of them. He turned and found himself looking into the fine features of his sister.

'Spoil things?' he queried.

'With the business,' she said, sticking her chin out mulishly. 'I saved it. You're not taking it from me.'

Blanco laughed. He had so much else on his mind, what with foreign legends and people trying to kill him and angels fighting each other, that he could quite honestly say that the family business was the last thing on his mind. He saw almost immediately that laughing had been a mistake. Angelica looked furious.

'How dare you laugh?' she said. 'It's because of you that father is ill! It's because of you that his business nearly collapsed and we were nearly put out on the street. And what would you have cared so long as you got to fly? You and your stupid dreams that are never going to come true.'

'Actually I did manage to fly,' said Blanco in a small voice, but she wasn't listening.

'Have you any idea how difficult it is to pretend to be a boy all day and then go back to being the dutiful daughter when I get home? Do you have any idea of how difficult it is to keep a business going? I've done it all and I've done most of it by myself and I'm not letting you come and take it all away from me now!'

'Angelica, shut up!' Blanco shouted, knowing that there was no other way he was going to be heard. She stopped her tirade but continued to look at him furiously.

'I promise you,' said Blanco, slowly and firmly, 'that I do not want to take over the business. That is one of the reasons why I went away in the first place.'

'Yes, and broke father's heart,' she said.

'Angelica,' he sighed, 'you can't have it both ways. Either you're glad I've gone because you get to take over the business or you're glad I'm back because I can help you with it.'

'I'm glad you went,' she said bitterly.

They stared at each other for a moment. They had never had much in common, they had always quarrelled furiously, but Blanco had never, until that moment, realized how much his sister actively disliked and resented him.

'I think you've done wonderfully,' he said placatingly. 'I couldn't have done it.'

'No, you couldn't,' she said. 'But how do I know that you won't change your mind about the business?'

'If it makes you feel any better,' said Blanco, 'I think I'm going to have to go away again.'

'Where?'

'I can't tell you.'

'You think it's clever being all mysterious like this. Well, it's not, it's stupid.'

Blanco shrugged. 'Angelica,' he said, 'why are you doing business with Señor Ferron?'

'Without him our business would have ended months ago. He saved us from losing everything. We've been working on a big trading venture together. It could make our fortune.'

'It doesn't have anything to do with lapis lazuli, does it?' asked Blanco.

'How do you know that?' she asked, looking stunned. 'It's a secret.'

Blanco hadn't known that, he had guessed, and it came as a bit of a shock to him to find that he was right. At the same time he wasn't totally surprised to hear it. Luca Ferron had obviously been plotting a lot while they had been in Malta: planning to marry Eva and tying up Blanco's family business.

'I've been invited to his wedding, you know,' said Angelica proudly. 'Not many people have so it shows how well he thinks of us. It's a secret. We're not even being told where it is until tomorrow.'

Blanco couldn't believe his luck.

'Will you take me to the wedding?' he asked.

She stared at him, her eyes full of suspicion and her look unfriendly, and then she nodded. 'You're still my brother even if you are annoying,' she said finally, a small smile breaking through her features. 'But you have to promise me that you won't disrupt the ceremony.'

Blanco laughed. 'Now how could I do that?'

Micha woke to find herself in a very strange place. It was dark and it smelt of rotting vegetation. When she tried to move she found that her hands, feet, and wings were bound. She tried to free them and couldn't. In addition her head

was aching. She managed to sit up and lean against the roots of the tree in which she was encased. She knew there was no way out unless she called on Azaz but if she did that, it would leave Eva unprotected. If she didn't, soon she wouldn't be able to breathe.

Blanco had continued walking after his sister had gone home. He had a lot of thinking to do and walking through the narrow little streets seemed the best way to do it. Before long, he found himself at the docks, looking at a familiar ship. He had last seen it at the docks in Barcelona and he knew that it belonged to Luca Ferron. There was a lot of activity on board. Lots of men rushing up and down the gangplank. Evidently Luca was planning to leave directly after the wedding.

Blanco was just about to turn away when he saw the last person he would have expected going up the gangplank. He looked more closely and then shook his head. He was obviously seeing things. He turned and headed into one of the little side streets. He had a wedding to prepare for.

Chapter 17

It really was a secret location. Just after midday a man appeared to escort Angelica to a gondola which would take her to the wedding. He looked surprised that she was to be accompanied but Angelica informed him in her most imperious tone that if her brother couldn't come then she wouldn't either. Having no orders to deal with such a situation, the man agreed.

The gondola was moored by their back steps and it was covered. When they stepped inside they found that the seats were luxuriously cushioned and there were little windows of coloured glass. While this meant that the inside was full of sparkling, coloured light, it also meant that it was impossible to see out.

'Isn't this lovely?' said Angelica as she settled herself on one of the velvet cushions.

Blanco nodded assent even as he began to wonder if he had walked into a trap. Luca must have suspected that Angelica would tell him about the wedding. What if he was being taken away from it rather than to it. He clutched his bag more tightly to him.

'What have you got in there?' asked Angelica.

Blanco smiled tightly. 'A present for the happy couple.'

* * *

Eva had never been so unhappy or so scared. She had tried refusing to leave her room that morning but her father had threatened to whip her. She got up but she had not given the servants any assistance in dressing her. It made no difference, for here she now stood at the church door, surrounded by her family, waiting for her bridegroom.

'Where are they all?' demanded Gump as he and Magdalena wandered around the living quarters of Blanco's home. The servant had informed them that there was no one in but Gump had insisted on looking for himself.

The servant looked a little unsure. 'The master and mistress have gone for a walk. The master had a bad night's sleep, which gave him an ache in the head, and he thought a little air would help. And then Signorina Angelica, or Signor, I never know what to call her now, she's . . .'

Gump looked at him impatiently and Magdalena intervened before Gump became even more irate.

'We're looking for Blanco,' she said. 'Do you know where he is?'

'Well, I was just coming to that,' said the servant, a trifle grumpily. 'He's gone off somewhere with his sister. It's some big secret.'

Gump stared at him steadily.

'Oh, very well, I admit it. I listened at the door. They're off to some wedding, but it's a big secret apparently.'

'Luca!' exclaimed Magdalena.

'Angelica must have been invited,' mused Gump. He

turned back to the servant. 'Where is it taking place? Where did they go?'

The servant shrugged his shoulders. 'That's because it's such a big secret,' he said. 'They didn't know where it was. Someone came for them in a covered gondola and off they went.'

Gump and Magdalena looked at each other.

'What do we do now?' asked Magdalena.

'You look lovely, Eva,' said Giuliana, squeezing her hand. 'Really lovely. I'm sure you're going to be very happy.'

Eva scowled at her, her look at odds with the glorious garments she wore. Her family and their friends and acquaintances lined the steps of the church and she was completely surrounded. Her father was determined that this would be a wedding that everyone would talk about with envy. There had been a lot of gossip and snide comments about his younger daughter over the years and he was delighted to have this opportunity to show off, in grand style, the fact that she had managed to make such a good match as the rich Luca Ferron.

Eva watched every gondola approach with trepidation, in case it was the one which carried her bridegroom. But her heart thumped as well, in case Blanco leapt out to save her. She knew that there was nothing he could do though. Not with all her family around. She looked up. Where were the angels? They were her only hope now.

Azaz was following Blanco and trying to tell him he was going the wrong way when he heard the call in his head.

It was a muffled call as though made reluctantly but he knew the voice instantly. He stopped following the gondola and listened more intently. Then he looked at the gondola and was torn. Would Blanco manage by himself?

Blanco realized that he had indeed walked into a trap when he popped his head out of the covered gondola and saw that they were circling the Dogana di Mare. He looked at the huge gondolier in charge of navigating the boat and then withdrew.

'Angelica,' he said conversationally, 'how much did Luca Ferron pay you to take me on this trip?'

Angelica gave him such a look of outrage that he knew immediately that she was guilty. He felt hurt and betrayed but he knew this wasn't the time to get angry.

'If you don't tell me where the wedding is taking place then I will tell father all about your little game,' he said as calmly as he could.

Angelica glanced at him.

'You wouldn't,' she said. 'It would break his heart.'

Blanco stared at her fixedly, convincing her that he meant every word he said.

'I knew that you would spoil things,' she said eventually. 'I wish you'd stayed away. The business will be ruined whether you tell father about me or I tell you about where the wedding is.'

'I'll sign something to say that the business is yours if you will tell me where the wedding is,' said Blanco after a pause.

Angelica looked at him in astonishment, trying to decide whether he meant it or not.

Blanco waited.

'How did you find out?' asked Magdalena as they hurried along through the crowds.

'Venice may look big compared to Malta,' Gump said, 'but it's a small town. Everyone knows everyone else's business. It's hard to keep a wedding secret here. But we must hurry. Those bells signify the wedding Mass is soon to begin.'

'*What are you doing here?*' murmured Micha when Azaz appeared in front of her.

'*You called me,*' he said, as he started to untie her bonds.

'*No I didn't,*' she said weakly. '*I deliberately didn't call you so that you would stay and look after Eva.*'

Azaz smiled at her. '*You may have thought you didn't call me,*' he said, '*but you did.*'

'*What about Eva?*'

The gondolier had had no time to react. He had been dreaming of his girlfriend when he felt a hard push from behind, followed by his legs being kicked from under him, and the next thing he knew he was in the canal. A splash beside him turned out to be the girl. She was yelling furiously but the gondola was already pulling away. He tried to swim after it but the girl clung to him. By the time he had stopped her from pulling him under the gondola was too far away to catch.

Blanco didn't feel the slightest twinge of guilt about pushing Angelica into the canal—even though he had promised her he wouldn't. He couldn't trust her and he had to get to Eva in time to stop her being married.

The church of Santa Maria Azura wasn't that far from where he was but he hadn't steered a gondola for years. At least he seemed to be moving in the right direction. The shouts of the two in the water got quieter and quieter and he began to think he might make it. Until the church bells began to ring . . .

Eva watched the groom's gondola approach with a gloomy heart. This was it, then. Neither Blanco nor the angels were coming to help her. She watched as the short, smiling figure of Luca Ferron got out of the golden boat and bowed to the cheering crowds. Everyone loved a wedding. He was followed by the Count. Eva gave a last despairing look around. No one was going to save her. She was going to have to marry the Stranger.

'We're going to be too late,' said Micha.
'We can only hope that Blanco isn't,' said Azaz.

Blanco could see the church across the canal and could even make out which of the figures on the steps was Eva. From his gondola he recognized, too, the short, squat figure of Luca Ferron climbing the steps with the tall, angular figure of the Count by his side, his silver cloak flowing behind him. Blanco wondered for a moment whether he had had a new one made or whether it still carried the three burn holes from their fight in Malta. But although he could see the wedding party he wasn't sure he would reach them in time.

Signor di Montini greeted Luca Ferron at the top of the steps. He was relieved to see him, having been terrified that he would be made a fool of in front of all his friends and business acquaintances if Luca hadn't shown up.

'May I say how beautiful you look, Eva?' said Luca, smiling at her with a taunting look in his eyes. 'Doesn't she, Maleficio?'

The Count was looking around, so sure was he that Blanco would materialize from nowhere and spoil things at the last moment. 'Oh, yes, of course,' he said hastily. 'Beautiful.'

Eva scowled at him and then saw a wing behind him. Her heart leapt for a moment until she realized that it belonged to Rameel.

'Where are my friends?' she demanded of him.

Her father began speaking loudly to cover the fact that his daughter was talking to thin air.

Rameel gave a smug smile. 'They are so sorry not to be here,' he said, 'but they do send their very best wishes and hope that you have a long and happy life with your husband.'

Luca took Eva's hand. She would have pulled away except that her father was standing behind her, pushing her arm forward so that she had no choice except to let Luca take it. His hand was hot and damp as he turned her to face the church doors—and the priest who stood there.

'Welcome,' said the priest, not looking Eva in the eye. 'Let us praise the Lord for this day. Let us pray.'

'Let's not,' said Luca pleasantly but firmly. 'Let's just start the ceremony.'

Chapter 18

Magdalena and Gump had finally managed to push their way through the crowd and had reached the bottom of the steps of Santa Maria Azura. The marriage ceremony was already under way.

'Does anyone here,' asked the priest, gabbling his words, obviously under orders to finish the ceremony as quickly as possible, 'know of any reason why these two people here present may not be wed?'

He paused only for a moment but it was long enough for Gump to make his voice heard.

'I do,' he shouted.

As one, the congregation on the steps above turned to look at him. The Count looked stunned, Luca amused, and Eva's father furious. Gump ignored them all and said, 'This marriage can't continue.'

'Don't believe anything he says!' shouted one voice. 'All he ever does is tell stories!'

'What is your reason?' asked the priest.

'The girl is a nun,' he said. 'She is promised to Christ.'

There were quite a few sharply drawn breaths at that and a loud murmuring began. Signor di Montini shook Eva and demanded to know if it was the truth. Eva nodded.

'It is true,' she said, trying to look demure and pious. The crowd gasped again.

'This woman here,' said Marco, pointing to Magdalena, 'is the abbess of the convent in Malta to which Eva is promised.'

'This is nonsense,' interrupted Count Maleficio crossly. 'Eva never took her vows and she never promised a dowry and therefore she is not a nun.'

'I want to be one though,' said Eva and someone halfway down the steps tried and failed to hide a laugh.

'Can we continue?' asked Luca, still smiling. 'My fiancée obviously has some friends who do not wish her to get married but I see no reason for that to stop a wedding. Or perhaps we should break with tradition and move inside the church and leave these people outside?'

Signor di Montini turned to the priest. 'Just get on with it,' he said. 'She's not a nun.'

'Yes I am!' said Eva loudly.

The priest hesitated. Gump and Magdalena didn't know what to do next.

'She is not a nun and she's not going to marry that man,' said another voice. The guests, delighted at all the excitement, turned to see who had spoken this time. The voice had come from the direction of the canals and there they saw a tall young man, standing in a gondola, with a determined look on his face.

'What now?' demanded Signor di Montini. Luca no longer looked so amused and the Count was only restrained from lunging at Blanco by the fact that there were so many people between them. Signor di Montini turned to Eva, who was looking delighted. 'Just how much shame are you intending to bring on this family?' He shook her.

'Take your hands off my wife!' shouted Blanco and everyone except the wedding party erupted with laughter.

'Oh, this is ridiculous,' said Luca. 'Maleficio, see off that young man, would you?'

'With pleasure,' said Maleficio, setting off down the steps with a murderous look in his eyes.

'I have proof!' said Blanco, waving a piece of parchment in the air.

Even Eva looked amazed at that.

Signor di Montini rushed down and tried to grab the piece of parchment. He couldn't quite reach the gondola.

'Who are you?' he demanded.

'I'm—'

'Blanco!' screamed Eva.

Looking up Blanco saw that Luca was trying to pull her away. He dropped to his knees, lifted something from the bottom of the gondola, put it to his shoulder and carefully took aim.

'Eva, get down!' he shouted. Eva threw herself on the ground as a streak of fire emerged from the end of the contraption that Blanco held against his shoulder. Count Maleficio turned at the shout and immediately wished he hadn't for his unmarked cheek was caught by the edge of the fiery rocket and he howled in outrage and pain as it scorched him. The crowd exclaimed in horror as the fire flew over their heads, most of them throwing themselves on the ground, praying as they did so. Luca tried to keep hold of Eva but she twisted out of his grip as he ducked to evade the fire.

In the mêlée which followed Eva crawled through the crowd and made her way to the canal. Blanco, who had been knocked down by the force of the shot, was trying to stop the gondola from capsizing. It swung wildly.

'What was that?' she gasped out.

He looked over her shoulder. Eva's father was just getting to his feet looking furious. Blanco grabbed her hand and pulled her aboard. 'I'll tell you later,' he said. 'We've got to get out of here.'

'You must be Eva,' said Gump, holding out his hand. 'I am very pleased to meet you officially, at last. I've heard a lot about you.'

'Are you . . . are you . . .' asked Eva, suddenly sounding very shy, 'are you Marco Polo?'

Gump nodded. 'Don't believe all the stories,' he said. He leaned forward and whispered. 'Only the ones I tell you.'

Eva laughed and started to understand why Blanco put such faith in his uncle to sort things out.

They were sitting in Bartolommeo the map-maker's shop. Blanco and Eva had managed to lose their pursuers but they couldn't risk going anywhere they might be found. Most of Venice was now looking for them but Blanco was fairly sure they wouldn't think of coming here.

'What was that thing you fired?' asked Eva. She knew it wasn't one of the miniature flying machines. It had looked much bigger and the fire was more ferocious.

Blanco looked at the ruined piece of metal which he had brought with him from the gondola.

'I'm not sure,' he said, turning it over in his hands. 'It was something I found in the Count's laboratory after he'd gone. He couldn't get it to work but I fiddled about with it on the ship and thought I'd give it a try.'

Eva looked at it. It was longer and broader than the

miniature flying machines and was made of metal, some of which was now twisted.

'So *are* you two married?' asked Gump.

'Of course not,' said Blanco. 'I can't understand,' he added, genuinely perplexed, 'why everyone wants to marry Eva.'

Eva scowled at him. Magdalena intervened.

'So what was the parchment?' she asked. 'It obviously convinced Eva's father.'

'Ah, that was me,' said Bartolommeo, coming out of the back quarters of the shop with a flagon of wine in his hand. 'I used to be a bit of a forger in my younger days. Marriage certificates are easy. Blanco came to me last night and I was able to make him one there and then.'

'Where have you been?' demanded Eva suddenly.

'I was out at the back,' said Bartolommeo a little nervously, for she had sounded very cross.

'I'm so sorry,' she said, turning to him. 'I wasn't talking to you. I was talking to them.'

Bartolommeo was none the wiser, for she was pointing at an empty corner of the room, but he was used to Gump bringing strange people to the shop and so he contented himself with pouring out the wine.

'I am sorry, Eva,' said Micha. 'Rameel captured me.'

'And I had to go . . .'

'Never mind all that,' said Eva. 'Have you two made up?'

They nodded.

'Then I forgive you,' she said magnanimously. 'Anyway, Blanco was there.'

Blanco blushed and, to cover his embarrassment, turned to Gump. 'What exactly are they after?' he asked.

Gump had been watching with fascination as Eva talked sternly to empty air but at Blanco's question he motioned to them all to sit down.

'It is time,' he said, 'that I told you the whole story. The letters hold a code.'

'Yes, yes, we know,' said Blanco impatiently. 'Magdalena explained it all on the ship.'

'Magdalena could not have explained it all,' said Gump, 'for she didn't know it all.'

Eva looked scared. She looked at Blanco but he was too busy looking at Gump, waiting for him to start, to notice her. Magdalena saw and put a comforting hand on her arm.

'When I was seventeen,' began Gump, 'I set off on a great adventure . . .'

'Oh, Gump,' said Blanco wearily. 'We all know this, or at least I do. I've heard you talk about your travels countless times.'

'Don't interrupt me, boy,' said Gump, sounding cross. 'Do you really think that I'm just going to cover old ground?'

Blanco grimaced but sat back quietly in his chair.

'We travelled first of all to Jerusalem and then onwards towards the East. Do you know, I've just thought, I wonder . . .'

'What?' asked Blanco.

'No,' said Gump thoughtfully, 'it probably doesn't matter. I've just remembered something that happened in Jerusalem but it doesn't have anything to do with this story.'

Blanco rolled his eyes in exasperation.

'After Jerusalem,' continued Gump, 'we passed through rough countries, difficult and dangerous to travel, and there were lots of problems to contend with. To make matters worse, I fell ill with a bad fever high in the mountains in a place called Badakhshan. My father and uncle left me there to recuperate while they went off on a trade mission. It was while I was there that I heard the legend.'

'But I thought the legend was false,' said Magdalena. 'I thought you had made it up in order to fool Christobal.'

'I was going to make one up,' admitted Gump. 'But then I remembered this one and I thought I would use it.'

'But what's the problem?' interjected Blanco. 'It's still just a legend, whether it was made up by you or by someone else.'

Gump's face made him fall silent.

'Have you heard the legend?' asked Gump. 'All of it?'

They all shook their heads.

'It's a simple story,' said Gump. 'The people of the mountains say that once there was a girl and a boy who were in love. One day a fallen angel came. He saw the girl and fell in love with her. But she loved the boy more than the angel. The angel killed the girl and took her heart and buried it deep in the earth and covered it with a mountain and then with a coat of ice. If he could not have her heart then neither could her lover. They say her heart turned to stone and became what it is now known as the heartstone. It is said that the heartstone is deep blue with red undertones but covered with a sheer face of clear ice—like an eye filmed with tears.'

They all sat in silence as Gump finished.

'But I still don't understand,' said Blanco. 'What is the heartstone? Why do they want it?'

'Because,' continued Gump, 'it was created with the powerful emotions of passion, love, jealousy, and regret, so the heartstone contains immense power. It is believed that anyone who holds it will have the power to change one thing. But it can only be freed by a special type of person. This was the bit I made easy for Christobal to decode, to distract him from our elopement letters. Of course, it didn't quite work out.'

Here he cast a quick look at Magdalena but she was staring fixedly at the floor.

'But what I don't understand,' said Blanco, 'is why now? If he's known about it for twenty years, why is he only trying to find it now?'

Gump looked down and Magdalena spotted it immediately.

'Marco?' she asked.

Gump looked up again. 'That really is my fault,' he said. 'When he was here last year, I taunted him with them. I said that there really was a heartstone and that the villagers in the mountains knew where it was. I told him that he would never be able to work out where it actually lay.'

'So that's why he stole the letters,' said Blanco. 'And that's why you asked me to get them back.'

'Well, I wanted them back anyway,' said Gump, quickly glancing again at Magdalena. 'They were very special to me.'

'But if you hadn't said anything last year,' said Blanco, 'then none of this might have happened.'

'Well . . .' started Gump.

'If you hadn't written them in the first place,' said Magdalena. 'If you hadn't tried to play games with him . . .'

'But I had to—' he started again, suddenly feeling that everything was his fault.

'But why do they think that I am the special person?' interrupted Eva in a low voice.

Gump turned to her. 'The rhyme runs like this:

> *To win this stone the Adept must*
> *First of all, fly like a bird*
> *Speak with the angels*
> *And love like no other . . .'*

'But why do they need Eva?' asked Blanco. 'Why can't they get it themselves? Luca can speak with the angels. He speaks to Rameel.'

'But he's not in love,' said Magdalena.

'The Count is in love,' interjected Eva, 'with you. And he can speak to Rameel too.'

'But he didn't fly,' Blanco pointed out. 'Only you and I did that.'

'But that means we could both do it,' said Eva. 'You can speak to Azaz.'

'Only if you're both in love,' said Gump gently.

Eva looked round at them all, her eyes falling finally on Blanco. She blushed scarlet as she took in the meaning of Gump's words.

'But I'm not,' she faltered. 'I mean . . .'

The embarrassment was too much for her and she stood up and rushed from the room. Blanco got up to go after her.

'No,' said Magdalena. 'Let me.'

Blanco was glad to let Magdalena take over and abruptly sat down again. 'So that's why Luca wants Eva,' he said. He shook his head. 'But it's just a legend. It can't be true.'

Gump leaned over and placed a hand on Blanco's

arm. 'It may not be,' he agreed, 'but the problem is that both Christobal and his friend Luca Ferron believe that it is and they will do everything to try to get Eva.'

'What are we going to do?' asked Blanco. He turned to Gump. 'You have to tell them that you made it up.'

'But I didn't,' he said calmly.

'So what can we do?'

Gump shrugged his shoulders. 'If I had had any idea that a joke I played twenty years ago to distract somebody would come back to haunt me like this then I would never have started,' he said helplessly.

'Well you did,' said Blanco bitterly, 'and now Eva's life is in danger.'

He was surprised at the depth of his anger but the thought of something happening to Eva scared him, more than he would ever have thought possible.

'That's not my fault,' said Gump. 'I never thought Christobal would be stupid enough to believe it and set off on a twenty year quest to prove it.'

'Then whose fault is it? If you and Magdalena had just eloped instead of writing about it then this would never have happened.'

Gump flinched at that. Since setting eyes on Magdalena again he had been thinking of what could have been. Neither of them had dared to bring it up with the other, focusing instead on the present. But Gump knew that it was a discussion that he could not run from for ever.

'That is not the point,' said Gump.

'Then what is?'

★   ★   ★

Lost in their argument, it took a long time for them to realize that Magdalena and Eva had not come back.

Blanco stared at the empty spot where Luca Ferron's ship had been moored the night before.

'They've gone,' he said rather unnecessarily to Gump since he could see the empty spot for himself. 'They must have taken them when they went outside. We should never have let them go, knowing that they were looking for Eva.'

'At least she has Magdalena to keep her company,' said Gump soothingly. 'And we know where they're heading.'

Blanco turned and stared at Gump. 'You don't understand,' he said coldly. 'I don't think that Magdalena has gone to help Eva. I think she handed her over to them.'

'What?' cried Gump in outrage. 'She would never do that. Why would you ever think that?'

'Because I saw her go up the gangplank of Luca's ship last night,' said Blanco. 'I just didn't believe the evidence of my own eyes.' He turned away.

'Where are you going?' asked Gump.

'After Eva.'

'You're an old man,' said Zia Donata.

'I'm still fit,' Marco replied indignantly, although he knew that his bones couldn't stand what they used to. 'Donata, I have to explain.' He hesitated, unsure how to continue. He had once, just before they were married, told her about Magdalena but he didn't know what to say now. 'About Magdalena. That's not why I'm going.'

'I know,' she replied.

'It's for the boy,' he said. 'I can't let him go alone.'

'That's one reason, I agree,' said Zia Donata. 'But you also have to go for another reason, Marco. You have to find out what you could have been.'

'You are a very wise woman and I love you,' said Marco.

'I'll still be here when you get back,' was all she said.

This time Blanco felt he had to say goodbye. He didn't think he should sneak off in the middle of the night again. He decided this before he discovered just how difficult goodbyes could be. His mother wept and wailed all over him and his father would not let go of his hand. Angelica was the only one who looked pleased.

'I told you I wouldn't interfere in the business,' Blanco said to her shortly.

'I know.' She hesitated and then, quickly, as though the words were forced out of her mouth against her will added, 'Good luck. May the angels look after you.'

Angelica didn't know about the angels so Blanco was surprised by her words but he nodded and smiled and accepted them with the grace with which they were offered. Neither of them were to know that, in the coming weeks, they were to prove a curse rather than a blessing.

Blanco picked up his travelling pack and turned to leave Venice for the second time. The journey he had begun so happily almost a year before was far from over.